DUELING THE DESPERADO

MIMI MILAN

EATON HOUSE

BRIDES OF BLESSINGS
Love More Precious Than Gold

DUELING THE DESPERADO

They could fight everything but love.

MIMI MILAN

Dueling the Desperado

© 2018 by Michele Claudio

This book is a work of fiction. Names, characters, businesses, organizations, places, events and incidents either are the product of the author's imagination or are used fictitiously. Any resemblance to actual persons, living or dead, events, or locales is entirely coincidental.

Cover design by Carpe Librum Book Design.

❀ Created with Vellum

What others are saying about Mimi Milan's books:

The Dancing Lady

Mimi Milan writes a beautiful story of two people saving each other and finding true love. Fina is one of the more secretive brides but there is also more to Nacho than simply owning the only restaurant in town. Can these two learn to trust each other and find love? Dive into this engaging holiday romance to find out!

~ CarterAndConnersMom, Reader ~

As I progress through the series I find myself drawn in more & more to the characters in Noelle. I appreciated the Spanish terms being explained naturally through the dialogue & they added "flavor" to the story. I would enjoy reading more books by this author.

~ ArmyMomX2, Reader ~

Full of surprises!
I couldn't figure out who had more secrets they were hiding,

Fina or Nacho? So glad there was a Happy Ever After to this book, I sure had my doubts at times!! If you're up for some creativity in the kitchen, you'll love this book!! I'm looking forward to reading more of Mimi's books!

~ Cindy Nipper, Reader ~

A Rebel in Jericho

"I thoroughly enjoyed A Rebel in Jericho. *I felt that it was a great read. The plot was interesting and kept me turning the pages to find out what would happen next. The characters were well developed and interesting. I enjoyed the historical aspect and the description at the end of real events hinted at in the story. I like that the ending lends itself well to a sequel while effectively completing this story. I can't wait to read more by this author.*

I love that 20 percent of the sales from this book goes toward stopping human trafficking which is a bigger problem than we realize."

~ Carrie, Reader ~

"A Rebel in Jericho has a little of everything for its readers to enjoy. Suspense, romance, deception, and the desire to survive. Catalina has an incredible strength within herself, while at the same time showing just how vulnerable she is. I was intrigued to find out what twist and turns would take place next with every

page I turned. I look forward to continuing reading this series and what other adventures are to come."

~ Warrior Ground ~

Twice Redeemed

I believe that this story is worth every bit of a five-star rating. It's worthy of winning a literary award."

~ Writer at Heart ~

This second book in the series is as good as the first. The characters are believable and well-written. Kind hearted former sheriff John Durbin needs to rescue the young woman who previously helped him. Will their relationship become more than rescuer and lady in danger? I recommend this book and the entire series.

~ Marianne Spitzer, Author ~

The Angel Paws Rescue series

"I really enjoyed all three of the novellas in this series (the Angel Paws Rescue series)*. Each novella is surprisingly very different*

from the other, but each has a wounded veteran and an arts person as the hero and heroine with a pet/service animal adopted from Angel Paws Rescue. I recommend the series to anyone who enjoys clean, heart-warming contemporary romance."

~ MH, Reader ~

To the ones still trying to claim their space ~

You belong.
You are home.

ACKNOWLEDGMENTS

There's a saying that writing is a lonely process. I'm not too sure I can agree with that. Perhaps the writing itself is done in private—and not even then is that always true. Oftentimes, there are fellow authors who like to gather (either in person or on social media) for writing "sprints." There are critique partners, editors, beta readers, cover artists, bloggers, marketing specialists and more. All of them play an important role in the course of producing a novel. I couldn't possibly name them all, but I would like to take a moment to recognize the few who did a fabulous job of helping bring *Dueling the Desperado* to life.

Always, I thank the Divine first for both the gift of story and the desire to sit down day after day to plug away at my computer. Sometimes the words are like molasses. They slowly pour out onto the page. Other times, they are like a geyser gushing forth with such urgency that I worry they will slip through my fingers. Slow or fast, peaceful or frantic, I am thankful for any way the Master Creator helps me find them.

I would also like to thank my editor, Patricia Highton.

Once again, you have made Eaton House a wonderful place to work. Thank you for finding the grammatical errors that my eyes continue to glaze over.

To my family and friends, thank you for all the support. Whether it's luncheons together or simply an encouraging comment on a social media post, you are invaluable and keep me going. I pray I can be there for all of you as you have all been for me.

To Evelyne of Carpe Librum Book Design, thank you for creating such a beautiful cover. It really brought my characters to life in a classic and timeless manner. I can't wait until we begin working together on the next cover for *Where the Snowy Owl Sleeps*.

To Guillermo, my husband and sometimes muse, thank you for all that you do to help this writing business grow. We writers are sometimes accused of being "weird sorts." So, *gracias* for accepting me in all my weird ways of midnight writing moments and addiction to cranberry scones and tea.

Last, but certainly never least, are the readers. I don't think there are words to express how much I appreciate all of you. The follows, emails, messages and "tags" on social media regarding the "next book" and your excitement to read it are inspiring. Whenever I feel like I'm dying of thirst in the writing desert, I receive an encouraging inquiry or read another good review and am ready to write again. Thank you so much for allowing me to share my stories.

PROLOGUE

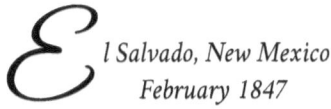 *l Salvado, New Mexico*
        February 1847

"CALIFORNIA? You can't be serious! That place is completely uncivilized."

Araceli Arroyo bit back a smile. Her friend, Georgia, had the tendency to over exaggerate whenever faced with dismaying news. "I believe you said something similar when you first arrived here in our little town."

Georgia feigned ignorance. "Did I? Well, I don't recall. Although, it would have been a truthful statement. It takes women like you and me – ladies of good virtue and strong character— to properly settle a place. Now who will help me run the *Society of Munificent Maidens*? Oh, Chel. Why do you have to move all the way to California?"

Araceli's mouth stretched into a thin, tight line. It did little to quell her irritation, though, and the slight Spanish accent that pricked her voice proved as much. "You know very well why I have to move."

Georgia's small gasp was followed by a moan of regret as she suddenly remembered her friend's plight. "Yes, how terribly rude of me. I'm so sorry, Chel. I didn't mean to be insensitive."

"Stop worrying, George. It's not your fault. It was those blasted soldiers who burned down our house and stole my family's land."

Araceli couldn't bring herself to say the rest of what had happened, but it didn't stop her mind from racing back to the day when American soldiers descended upon the Arroyo hacienda in search of her brothers—soldiers fighting for the Mexican army. The two youngest had indeed returned home and, after being tracked and discovered, were promptly executed. Her older brother, Pedro, never made it back at all. It was a sure sign the war across the border had greedily devoured him like so many others.

Like everything else she cared for.

She forced back the memories filled with smoldering remains of flames licking at the grand hacienda her father had built with his own two hands—a wedding gift to a mother who parted the world with grief in her heart when the war first came and all three sons marched off together.

Araceli cleared her throat and gave the woman before her a small embrace. The Southern socialite latched her long, milky white arms around Chel's shoulders in return, squeezing tightly.

"I will miss you dearly, my girl. You must promise me that you'll paint the California coast. Mind you, I'll take nothing less than your greatest masterpiece for my office."

"I don't think we'll be going that far," Araceli said with a sad smile. "The town my father picked out is a place called Blessings. He believes God will grant us good fortune if we settle in a town with a name like that."

"And you, Chel? What is it that you believe?"

There is no God.

The words almost slipped from her mouth, but a sour impression was the last thing she wanted to leave her friend with. So, she only gave the woman a nonchalant shrug and said, "*Sabe?* Who am I to say, George? I believe life is what you make of it... and I intend to make the most out of California."

"That's the spirit!" George grabbed one hand and gave it a reassuring squeeze. "You'll be sure to go far with an attitude like that—maybe even so far as the California coast."

George gave her a wink then and touched the side of her nose—a small gesture the women used with one another to indicate a knowledge they shared. In this instance, George wished a painting of the sea. Araceli had never been one to turn down an adventure.

Why start now?

Someday she would end up on the golden coast—one foot buried in the gleam of pale yellow sand, the other planted in the churning tide—and she would collect her paints and capture that moment for her friend and confidant.

That is, if she ever got ahold of more paints.

"I better go," she finally said. "My father said we're catching tomorrow's coach and there's still plenty of packing to do."

"Will you need any help? With the packing, that is."

Araceli shook her head. "You're kind to offer, but I'm sure we'll manage."

"Very well. Be sure to write me as soon as you get to this —what did you call it? Blessings? Yes, that was it. I want to know you've arrived safely."

"You know I will," Araceli said and the women embraced one last time. Then she climbed onto her horse and took the road heading away from George's quaint cottage with its large sitting porch and white picket fence gallantly dressed in wild daisies growing from base to hem. Araceli thought about those flowers long after the house and her friend had fallen from view, feeling as wild as those blooms looked. There were days when great sadness engulfed her and she questioned the ability to even rise from her bed; the curtains remaining drawn on yet another dreadful day. Then the pendulum of emotions would swing in the opposite direction, filling her with enough energy to take on an invading army with little more than the swish of a horse-haired brush dipped in the colors of creation.

Except she had no colors now.

All that remained of her precious paints were squirreled away in a lonely spot back in her family's burnt home. She looked west and dared to toy with the idea... Would it be safe to return? Her father had warned her to never venture the roads leading back to the ranch they once owned—that there was no guarantee the soldiers had dispersed despite the war ending. Besides, America had claimed victory and the Mexicans who lived on the north side of the new border were now in the precarious position of not really belonging anywhere. They had yet to be granted American citizenship, making it easy for the government to lay claim to lands that boasted generations of hard work and inheritance. That is what had come to pass for her own family. With brothers fighting for what was (politically speaking) the wrong side, the family was deemed traitorous. *A miracle*, her father had declared when they were given the option to abandon the homestead. However, she was away that day on one of her usual explorations as was custom whenever she felt the well running dry. She escaped into nature to seek out its beauty and secrets that it would offer up only to those who learned to patiently wait for great revelations.

She could do that once again.

With the sun kissing the horizon, a promise on its lover's

4

lips bespoke of the night soon to be born. Araceli turned her horse down the forbidden road to wait for it.

～

"AIN'T NOTHING grown here but a bunch of Mexican strawberries."

The comment brought a round of laughter from several of the soldiers as they sat around the campfire, pitching dried beans at one another. Miguel Santiago chuckled with the rest of them, but the sound that reached his ears was nothing more than a reflection of how he felt inside.

Hollow.

He hated this war and the way they had seized this ranch, but most of all he hated himself. Angry and fearful at the same time, he would never admit that he was what his men hated most.

Mexican.

Well, half Mexican, that is. With an American mother and Mexican father—neither of whom he had ever known—he grew up on a plantation owned by grandparents who did their best to teach him how terrible his father's people, supposedly from Puebla, really were. However, despite their abhorrence for Mexicans, their field hands consisted of foreign labor because they worked hard and cheap and provided something of a clear conscience for his grandfather that he did not run *that* kind of business—the one that chained men or whipped them. His workers were paid employees after all.

Miguel—or Michael, as his grandparents had insisted—grew up working alongside them. It gave him an education he never expected would be of much use, namely, that of speaking Spanish accompanied by the knowledge of Mexican culture, history and geography. That was one of the reasons the army took him in so quickly. Although, the truth was they happily took in any male capable of shooting down a perceived threat. However, he didn't want them treating him different from any other comrade and knew he could get by on his fair looks. So, he told them only the greatest highlights. He was Michael St. James (the English translation of his paternal surname) and kin to Daniel Delacroix of the Louisiana Delacroix. Yes, he would gladly serve his country, provided he was given a land grant in exchange for his military service. Of course, he would be more than willing to run off any resistance in order to claim his bounty, be it the decimation of a thousand men or only two young curs who abandoned the Mexican army in pref-erence of returning to the only home they ever knew. Thankfully, he had been in town that day and wasn't the one to call *fire!*

Fire.

The thought of the word reminded him of the burning building he happened upon— another of his men's indiscre-tions, which were less than appreciated. Yet, again, they did the very thing he was thankful he had not been called upon to do—rid the hacienda of its occupants. So, neither the blood nor burning were truly on his hand. That was the explanation he used to reassure himself that he was within his right to claim this land—the fact they did not occur on his watch. Therefore, the responsibility was not his—only the ranch and he would have it any way he could if it meant never returning to his grandfather's home again. His only hope was that he would find enough peace to stay on it.

"What the—"

He looked up when a bean popped off the side of his face.

One of the men gave him a sheepish grin. "Sorry, captain. We were just checking to see if you were alive."

"Yeah, you looked like you might have gotten lost in there

somewhere," another chimed before taking a swig from his bottle of whiskey.

Miguel stood and brushed himself off. "You boys better stop passing around that joy juice and get some sense. We'll be taking turns on watch tonight."

"Aw, I don't get why we can't just sleep in the house," the soldier said and took another drink.

"Captain's done told ya why before. Say one of them Mexi-*cans* get it in their head that they don't much like being pushed off their land. They might come in here ready to blow holes in our jaws, ya big dummy."

"I ain't no dummy, you ugly piece of—"

"Miller! Grey!"

Both men jumped at Miguel's strong bark. The other men in camp—a total of twelve— quieted as well. It was good to have their attention, but better to have their trust.

"I'll take the first watch," he said. He walked over to his horse and reached into the saddle, pulling out a sack that contained a handful of day-old biscuits and a hunk of salted meat wrapped in cloth. Knowing the men would be more considerate to the one passing out the food, he tossed it to the youngest in the group, a quiet youth the others had dubbed "Buffalo Boy" due to a rumor that he was half Apache. "Pass it around and get some real food on your stomachs."

The boy smiled briefly and then grew serious, nodding a confirmation that he could be trusted with the task. Satisfied, Miguel turned on his heel and marched away, hopeful the time alone would be enough to clear his mind as he followed an old path back towards the hacienda he had laid claim to. Miguel found some comfort in the way the edifice stood tall against the darkening skies. It very much reflected the path his own life seemed to take. He wished to become something grand, but remained weighed down by a darkness he could

7

not change. It was a dark veil so profound that he almost couldn't distinguish it from his surroundings, and had there not been the snap of a twig and rustle of soft steps on dead grass, he would never had seen the slender figure that slipped into the hacienda on his watch.

Not on *his* watch!

Hand on his sidearm, Miguel quietly—much more so than the trespasser—made his way to where the intruder had dared to enter. He debated for a moment that a wise man would call for the rest of the troop, but then reasoned that half of them were too drunk to be of any real use anyway... and was he so weak that he couldn't handle one lone squatter on his own? A boy no less? Judging from the height and build, that is who broke into the homestead now. Yes, Miguel could easily diffuse this situation.

He peered into the building, quietly entering the empty main hall, and stood ramrod still—waiting for some sign that he had not imagined it after all. Thankfully, he was not disappointed and a tinkling noise like that of crystal touching glass sounded from a nearby hallway. He carefully approached it to find a soft glow from a room at the opposite end, confirming his suspicion that some adolescent was probably looking for a place to hang his hat for the night. It would have to be someplace else, though. Miguel hadn't run off the last occupants only to abandon his goal a week later by allowing some young gun to do the same to him. When the treaty between Mexico and America was put into effect, he would be standing right here—feet firmly planted in a place that he could call his own, work according to *his* will and maybe even pass on to the blood that wanted to be tied to him.

He peered around the threshold and his mind boggled.

There – in one corner of the softly decorated study—was a woman in a pair of boy trousers and dark fitted blouse. He could hardly make her out in the dim light, but she stood in such a way that there was no mistaking her gender. She appeared to be calmly examining small glass jars all lined up on a desk beside a large wood frame supporting a blank crème colored canvas. Miguel wasn't sure which fact surprised him more— that there was a woman unconventionally dressed or that she carried on her task as though it were the most natural thing in the world.

"What do think you're about?" he blurted.

The woman spun around, her eyes wild. She raised the jar in her hand, bringing it back behind her head only to swing her arm forward and then suddenly stopped. She glanced down at the jar with a look of mixed emotions. With a sigh of resignation, she placed it in a satchel she carried and then faced him again, her hands planted on her hips.

"Are you blind or ignorant?"

"What?" Miguel sputtered.

The woman stepped forward, the light shining onto her face enough for him to make out her flared nose. A bit of anger stained her voice. "Didn't you ask me what I'm doing? Only someone blind or boorish wouldn't be able to figure it out. Since you're staring at me with eyes that look ready to roll out of your head, I can only assume it must be the latter."

What in the—

The sound of irritated tapping brought Miguel's attention down to her feet where one boot anxiously rapped the floor. He slowly dragged his gaze upward. Despite her obvious irritation, she was quite a sight to behold. His eyes were adjusting to the gentle glow of the lamp she had lit, and he could see her features well enough now to know that her long lashed, brown slanted eyes would be engraved on his mind forever. He searched the rest of her sun-kissed face and decided that he found the rest of it pleasing as well. From her full lips to her arched brows and all the way up to the coiled braid wrapped around her head like a crown, he was positive she was the kind of woman that could turn his head every time.

"You need to leave."

The words came out gruffer than he had intended. Her eyes drew into angry slits.

"This is *my* house," she hissed. "*You* are the one who should be leaving."

Her words set him back with the realization that she was part of the family they had forced from the land. That meant that she was also related to the two Mexican soldiers his men had killed. Part of him felt sorry for her. The other part had no remorse whatsoever. While she herself was innocent of any wrongdoing, her family had housed traitors who had stolen important documents from one of his generals. His expression hardened.

"Like I said, you should leave."

She refused to be intimidated. "I'll have you know I hate American soldiers."

"Well, that's a pity because I'm rather positive my men would love to make your acquaintance. It's been a long time since any of them have had the pleasure of a woman's company."

She gasped, making him feel as dark as the shadows he still stood in.

"Good. You get it now. This place is too dangerous for a face like yours."

"I only wanted my paints."

The tender resignation in her voice tugged at his chest in a way he hadn't felt before. "Well, go on and collect your things. I'll stand watch."

"Thank you."

He was unprepared for her gratitude and the look of appreciation she graced him with. He wanted to say more and opened his mouth to do so, but then snapped it shut again. He gave her a solid nod. With lead filled feet he forced himself to head back outside. He reluctantly made his way towards camp, counting seconds that rolled into minutes until he felt sufficient time had passed. He was sure she was gone now.

Yet in some strange way she remained with him.

 lessings, California
Summer 1851

"TELL ME, *hija*. What was wrong with that one?" Don Arroyo sat back in his desk chair and calmly folded his rough, withering hands. "It's the third proposal you've turned down in the past year. The first I could understand and, perhaps, even the second. But this time? This was Caleb Strauss. It doesn't get much better than that. For all that's holy... he owns the bank, Chelita!"

At the sound of the pet name, Araceli knew she could easily win her father's forgiveness and cracked a large smile. However, a frown drew his troubled brows together and every trace of her amusement was effectively scoured away. She hung her head with feigned contrition.

"I'm sorry, Papa. I promise I will do better."

"That's what you said the last time. Now you run off one of the most influential people who could help our business grow—not to mention care for you once I leave this world."

"*Ay, Papa*. Stop talking like that. You're not going anywhere any time soon—and you know it.

"*Si te toca, te toca.*"

Araceli refrained from rolling her eyes at the tired "if it's your time to go" Mexican saying, and crossed the room to where her *robozo* hung off a nearby hook. She wrapped the colorful shawl around her shoulders, determined that she would not fall into her father's snare like she did the last time. Feeling guilty for showing little interest in the preceding gentlemen before Strauss, she agreed to at least dinner at the Arroyo home with them. Each night had been filled with never-ending chatter about potential business opportunities that could change the world with help from a man like her father. Thankfully, Juan Arroyo was not the sort to be easily taken in.

Neither was Araceli.

She rejected her father's petition as easily as he disregarded her claim that she was already married — loyal to no other but the visions she created with the flick of her wrist.

"Really, father. You would think I was a terrible burden. Is my cooking so bad? I know it isn't as enticing as whatever it that Priya woman conjures up on the Sundays you spend away from home, but at least you know what's in it." Her father sputtered at the sound of the young, widowed washwoman's name—Araceli's proof that he didn't really believe he would die any time soon since they were secretly courting. "You know where my heart belongs. Now, I'm off to satisfy it. I'll be by the mill in a while to see to the books."

She gave him her most dazzling smile followed by a blown kiss delivered off the palm of her long, slender fingers. *Artist's hands*, her father had beamed with pride when telling the first would-be suitor of her talent. Señor Arroyo didn't seem so proud at the moment, though. He only sighed with resignation and waved her off, his face plagued with worry.

Araceli hated to see him so, but she refused to marry for anything less than love to a man who understood her heart belonged to her art—and the likelihood of finding such in their small town of limited choices was less than likely. Her father knew that, too. Still, he sat at his desk only partially unaffected by her charm. He finally gave her a smile, his head shaking as he chuckled.

"*Ay*, Chelita. What am I going to do with you?"

Satisfied that she had won the battle, Araceli returned the smile and hiked out of the room. She snatched up a satchel prepared earlier. It was filled with fewer jars of paint than she wished, but Blessings was a small town and colors were more difficult to come by than in a large city. Add to that the mountains and river that surrounded them and the location became quite remote, making the stage that carried in goods much slower than in other places.

Like El Salvado.

From time to time, Araceli's mind still wandered back to the New Mexico home she had known most of her life. It wasn't often, and she was thankful for that, because she truly did enjoy the new living she and her father had carved out for themselves. Still, every now and then, something would tug at the corners of her mind and dredge up bittersweet memories. Her older brother, Juan, pushing her on a makeshift swing hanging from an old Ash tree with branches as strong as the legs of any one of her brothers who could outrun her no matter how hard she tried. Before painting had become her everything—the reason for continuing to push air in and out of the dusty old lungs that seemed to have dried up along with her heart—most days had been spent in practice to learn to run faster. Her skirts would always wrap themselves around her legs, though, tripping her every attempt to best the boys. Of course, mama was alive then and no amount of pleading would have her agree to Araceli's desire to wear trousers like her brothers did.

The recollection burned bright and she wondered what her mother would think to see her daughter sport such fashions during midnight rendezvous to capture the presence of an owl or other wildlife that only ventured out when the rest of the world slept. Then again, what would her father think?

Araceli shuddered at the possibilities and continued on towards town, inhaling deeply. The air promised a summer full of wonder and she was more than eager to discover what delights the universe held out to her. Would she find a perfect orange sky to paint? Perhaps an owl would lead her back to its nest, where a trio of owlets waited to grace the world with their presence. Yes, dreaming about painting was almost as good as the deed itself at times.

"There you are."

Araceli twisted around to find one of her good friends approaching her, and smiled. She greeted her with a customary embrace, briefly pressing one cheek against her friend's face. "*Hola*, Maxine. *Cómo estás?*"

"*Muy bien*," Maxine giggled. "How did I do?"

"Very well. Keep practicing and I'm sure you'll speak Spanish better than me in no time."

"Oh, you're just being generous. I know I don't quite have the accent down yet."

"But you will soon," Araceli encouraged her. "Anyone who can keep books the way you can has the world as a pearl in her oyster."

"Are you a poet or a painter?" Maxine teased.

"Both today."

"Well, someone's in a grand mood."

"Hmmm… Not quite grand, but I do have some reason to celebrate." Araceli gave her friend a confident nod. "I do believe my father and I have finally reached an understanding."

"Oh? What kind would that be?"

"I am going to remain a free woman. That is, if yesterday's little flop with Mr. Strauss paired with this morning's conversation is any indicator."

"Really?" A playful look crossed Maxine's face. "Then I suppose you wouldn't be the least bit interested in the latest cowpokes that arrive in town."

"Not in the least." Curiosity got the better of Araceli. Thoughtful, her pace slowed. "Just arrived?"

Maxine eagerly nodded, an expectant look on her face as she waited for her friend to respond appropriately. "A couple of riders came in about an hour ago. Said they passed the coach, too. So, that might mean even more newcomers within the hour."

Araceli examined her dress and deemed it suitable.

"Oh, alright. We're already rag ready. Let's grab a quick bite at the café and then go find out what we can... but only to see what new blood is in town. It's not like either of us would actually be interested in one of those *guajolotes*."

"What does that one mean?" Maxine zealously inquired. She laughed when her friend assertively answered.

"Turkeys."

CHAPTER 2

The smell of dust drifted on the air as the stagecoach set off once again, hauling with it a bag of mail and a disgruntled couple who continued to complain that it was taking the driver far too long to reach San Francisco. There wasn't much Miguel was thankful for considering the world seemed intent to deliver him the short straw time and again, but he did deem it nothing short of a miracle that he survived the long trip west with the brooding pair. From the bits and pieces Miguel had gathered from sporadic spats, the man's uncle had left him with quite an inheritance —provided the man could prove he had renounced his "sinful" ways and settled down. With a deadline to claim the inheritance approaching, what else could the fellow do except marry the first lady he came upon? Unfortunately, neither one cared much for the other, each making it known to all who cared to listen.

Miguel chuckled and counted his blessings.

Blessings.

It was mighty peculiar to find himself in a town with the

same moniker. Slinging his satchel of meager belongings over his shoulder, he scratched at his beard—a new addition to his appearance that he still debated on removing. The extra hair was good for hiding half his face, but it was itchier than a patch of poison oak on a dry summer day.

He put the irritating itch out of his mind and looked over his surroundings. Hopefully it wasn't overrun by some religious nuts—not that he had a problem with God or anything. He believed in the boss man. He just didn't think it was a good idea for the two of them to get too close to one another. Yep, Miguel liked God like he enjoyed women—from afar. Anything more was just inviting trouble.

"Michael!"

The sound of his American name spun him around.

"Well, if it ain't the dog that drew first. Put it there, Pete."

Miguel stuck his hand out and grabbed hold of the outstretched one his long-time war buddy offered. The two men enthusiastically shook hands before briefly embracing, patting one another on the back. Pete let out a loud whoop.

"Now, don't you go telling stories, boy." He gave Miguel a wink. "I don't think my wife would care much for them."

Upon the address, a woman stepped forward. She held a dainty hand out to him. "Pleased to meet you. My name's Pati."

Miguel's eyes grew wide. He craned his head towards his old friend. "You didn't say nothing about getting married!"

Pete smiled sheepishly. "Yeah, well, this town has a funny way of doing things like that."

Miguel highly doubted that was true. At least, he did in his case. He couldn't fault Pete for falling for the pretty brunette with a distinct Irish accent—the last fact a sticking point that immediately carried him back to the fields where he found Irishmen fighting alongside Mexicans, leaving him to momentarily wonder at the time as to whether or not he was fighting on the right side.

Pete cleared his throat, forcing Miguel out of his reverie. He shook his head and grasped Pati's hand. "Excuse me, ma'am. I plumb forgot my manners. Name's Michael St. James."

"Not to worry," she smiled kindly. "Men and women alike forget them on the trail."

She raised a brow, turning slightly towards her husband. Pete's smile grew at some private knowledge the two of them shared. Feeling like an intruder, Miguel shifted, his hand dropping back to his side. He turned away and glanced up and down the main street. "Well, looks like a nice enough town."

"Oh, it is. I can guarantee you that," Pete said. "The folks around here are real nice, and like I wrote in my letter, there's more than enough work to go around. In fact, I'm sure Winslet Atherton would be more than happy to set you up with something steady in one of his mines."

The thought of possibly being trapped in a mine was less than appealing, but work was work and his empty pockets were telling him it was about time to be finding some. "That sounds right fine. If you'll just point me in the right direction, then I'll be happy to talk to this Atherton fella."

"Don't you want to settle in first?" Pati asked, surprised.

"She's right, buddy. You just got in and considering the company that just left, I can't imagine it was an easy ride. We can take a ride up to the house—give you a chance to freshen up if you'd like."

Miguel smiled to hide the idea that he didn't like the idea of staying with Pete. It wasn't that he had a problem with the man—they had been comrades in the war and friends ever since. He just didn't like the idea of intruding. A newly married couple needed their own space. "That's a mighty nice enough offer, friend, but I ain't no dandelion yet. I think I'd just like to dig in and get to work... leave the resting for the young, old and newlyweds, if you know what I mean."

Understanding registered on Pete's face, followed by a slight color of embarrassment. He chuckled. "I hear ya, partner. At least allow us to take you to lunch, though. We've got a fine little place called the Forty-Niner Café. They've got just about anything you can imagine there."

"Yes," Pati enthusiastically agreed. "I wouldn't mind visiting for myself and seeing what sweets Roxie created this week."

"Roxie?"

"She's the cook at the café," Pete explained. "Works for a guy named Paul León. Nice enough fellow, but Roxie's the real favorite whenever she makes a new batch of chocolates."

"They are delightful," Pati agreed.

Miguel smiled. He had a real sweet tooth and it had been a long time since he'd tried anything like chocolate. "Well, I've never been the sort to turn down a good meal. Don't see the sense in starting now. Lunch sounds like a pretty good idea to me."

His friend patted him on the back. "Great! It's just at the end of Main Street, across from Pullen House."

Miguel ambled alongside Pete and his wife. "That a boarding house of sorts?"

"More like a swanky hotel."

Swanky? That sounded a little above Miguel's pocket. He shook his head. "Fine chocolates and fancy hotels. Not exactly the sort of things I'd have thought to find in a small mining town."

"Well, Winslet's been setting up here for a while. He's real generous, too. Doesn't mind helping out folks whenever he can and encourages the town to grow—especially for those who left behind lives of luxury."

Miguel nodded in agreement, but the wheels in his mind had already started turning again. *A life of luxury.* He had never really known such a thing. Even though his grandfather was one of the wealthiest around, he made sure Miguel remembered his place. That included the fact that he might have had his mother's blood, but he still had his father's Mexican heritage too. That didn't make him quite good enough to carry the Delacroix name.

"There it is." Pete pointed to a small building of clapboard and modest windows, a wooden walkway lined along the front side of it.

"Looks good," Miguel said as they approached the building. He nodded at a pair of roughriders leaving the building, but then quickly ducked his head when they seemed a little too familiar.

Just to be safe.

Pete led the way inside, pausing momentarily as he entered. He made a show of taking in a strong whiff of the air. "Ah, almost as good as home. Almost."

Pati gave him a playful nudge before moving away. "I'm off to see Roxie and find out what treats she has. Go ahead and order for me. You know what I like."

Pete gave her a nod and grabbed a table for them to sit at. Miguel followed, noting that the diner seemed to do good business. Most of the tables were full.

"I've got to admit, I never thought I'd see the day when you were tied up. It seems to suit you, though."

"Yes, sir, it does. I can't imagine what my life would be like now without Pati in it. Blessings surely did just that— bless me beyond anything I could have ever imagined."

"Well, I'm hoping for the same—a blessing that is. I'll take mine in the form of some solid cash, though. I'm not at all interested in marriage."

"Never say never," Pete advised. "Stranger things have happened."

"Maybe so," Miguel agreed. "However, I'm not about to let them happen to me."

He would have continued, but Paul León approached their table and the conversation died down. Pete made the appropriate introductions and then ordered for him and Pati.

"That sounds pretty good," Miguel said. "It's been a while since I've had any decent spoon bread. I'll take some with my steak—medium rare."

"And to drink, señor?"

Miguel's brow shot up at the sound of Spanish being spoken to him. "*Señor*? Now why would you go and call me that?"

Confusion marred the café owner's face. "My apologies, sir. I occasionally slip back into my native language."

Miguel felt a bit like a heel for being so suspicious and jumping to conclusions. How would anyone in this small town know his true heritage? "No need to apologize. Just remember this is American country now. Might not do so well to speak Spanish around some folks."

"Of course," Mr. León agreed, apprehension still plagued his features and he shot a look of concern at Pete. "If you'll excuse me, I'll go get your lunch."

Pete nodded, smiling. As soon as the owner walked away, he turned to Miguel. "Hey, you don't have to worry about anything here. This town's not like that."

"Maybe not, but I'd rather not take any chances. You haven't told anyone nothing about me. Have you?"

"What do you take me for? A rat? I ain't said nothing about your past—on either account."

23

Miguel sat back, only slightly relaxed. He didn't like the idea of people knowing his heritage—didn't want them judging him for it. However, the only thing that put a quake in his boots was the thought of someone catching on to the reason he pulled up out of New Mexico. He wasn't about to be pinned for a crime he didn't commit!

"That would be lovely. Thank you, Roxie."

Pati joined them again and Miguel couldn't help but wonder if his friend had shared their secrets with his wife. He raised a questioning brow at Pete who slightly shook his head with a negative, allowing Miguel to once again relax.

"Roxie has just agreed to be on the welcoming committee," Pati happily reported. "She'll be donating a small box of chocolates to any newcomers taking residence in Blessings. Of course, that will include you as well, Mister St. James. However, it'll take a day or two since she doesn't have any on hand at the moment."

"That's unusual," Pete said as Mr. León approached, carrying a small tray of glasses filled with lemonade. "I've never known her to actually run out of sweets before."

Paul León sat a cup down in front of Miguel, who marveled at the orange, lemon and lime slices garnishing the glass rim.

Fancy indeed.

He picked up the beverage and took a sip, delighting in the sweet mixture. "Well, if those chocolates are even half as good as this, then I'm sure to become a regular customer."

"Not if Bart Frister has anything to do with it," Paul groused. *"Como un Don Juan, todo el mundo se olvidó."*

The digging remark about the wishful ladies' man caught Miguel by surprise. He tried to swallow down his laughter despite the mouthful of lemonade. The results were disastrous. He coughed and spurted, wiping at his wet nose and tearing eyes. Several patrons chuckled, but it was the soft laughter from a nearby table that caught his attention. His mouth went dry to find an olive washed beauty boldly staring back at him. Amusement shone in her eyes until the woman she was dining with tapped her arm, making her quickly sober.

"You alright, partner?" Pete asked.

"Yeah, yeah. I'm fine. Just hit a sour spot is all." Miguel looked up to catch a disbelieving glare from the owner, and he quickly rushed on. "Or maybe I just swallowed wrong."

The owner sniffed disapprovingly. "The food should be ready. If you'll excuse me… sir."

The way he stressed the word caused Miguel to inwardly cringe. Not even a day in town and he was already off on the wrong foot. He leaned towards Pete and whispered, "I think I might have made a bad impression with that León fella."

"What? Paul? Nonsense. He's harmless—you'll see."

Miguel wasn't too sure he agreed, but didn't think it was to say such—especially when the man crossed the room with yet another tray and set a plate of steaming food down in front of him.

"Much obliged," he said and cut into his steak. "This looks perfect."

The compliment earned him a nod of appreciation and the man went off again, smiling, to see to other matters.

"See? That wasn't so hard," Pete encouraged him. He seemed ready to say more, but the front door to the café swung open and caught his attention. "Well, if it isn't the man himself. This here is the man I was telling you about. Michael, this is Winslet Atherton."

Miguel moved to stand, but Winslet motioned him back down. "No need to trouble yourself, son. In fact, it gives me an excuse to sit myself down for a spell. That is, if y'all don't mind me joining in for a glass of something cool to drink."

"We'd be delighted, Mr. Winslet." Pati gave the elderly

man her best smile. He awarded her with one of his own, not the least bit bashful that a few teeth were missing.

Winslet grabbed a chair from a nearby empty table and pulled it up to join them. He stuck his hand out to Miguel. "Allow me to properly introduce myself now. Atherton Winslet, prospector and protector in this little piece of paradise, at your service."

"Good to meet you, sir. Name's Michael St. James and I'm just your run-of-the-mill cowpoke, looking to see what the west has to offer."

"Well, Blessings has plenty, that's for sure. Maybe you can tell us more about yourself and we can see where you might fit in best."

"Yes, Mister St. James," Pati finally spoke after taking a sip of her lemonade. "My dear Pete hasn't shared much more than the fact the two of you served together in the war. Is that right?"

"Indeed, ma'am." Miguel looked her way and caught a glare from the pretty lady who had laughed at him just a few minutes earlier. The searing look in her eyes made him feel like he was on trial for committing the worst imaginable crime. He cleared his throat, quickly cutting into his steak and shoving a forkful of the meat in his mouth, barely chewing or tasting it as he swallowed past the lump in his throat. "I'm afraid there's not much more to tell. It was an unfortunate time for everyone involved."

He busied himself with chewing, hopeful she wouldn't ask any more questions and was thankful when Pete spoke up instead.

"Thankfully, that was a long time ago. Now you've arrived and I'm sure Mr. Winslet here wouldn't mind taking you on at the mines."

"Well, I'm not too sure." Atherton sat back and scratched

at his scraggly beard. "Kind of thinking we're at quota right now."

"At quota?" Pete asked, surprised.

"Yep," Atherton insisted. "I think that's about right. I mean, maybe we are and maybe we ain't. I don't feel right about taking the risk in case we are, though. I wouldn't want to hire ya on just to let ya go again—or worse—have to lay off one of the old timers who've been loyal since we was digging out nothing but dirt. Nope, it wouldn't be right. Besides, you don't look much like a mining man to me at all. No, sir. Might be better suited for some other kind of work, though."

Miguel perked up. "Oh, yeah? What kind of other work?"

"How do you feel about sawmills?"

A sputtering sound came from across the dining room and the pretty lady who had previously attracted Miguel's attention bolted up from her seat, dropped a bill on the table and excused herself from her company.

"What's with her?" Miguel mumbled.

Pete opened his mouth to speak, but Mr. Winslet gave him a soft kick under the table. He smiled up at Pete and slyly winked.

"Oh, that's just Miss Chel. She's one of those creative sorts—big into painting and such. You know how they are."

Miguel didn't know how they were, but something about paint tugged at the alcoves of his mind. "Well, I hope everything's alright for her."

"I'm sure she's fine," Atherton insisted. "Now let's get back to what we were discussing."

"Yes, you were telling me something about working at a sawmill. I think I'd like that. In fact, I believe I'd rather enjoy it a great deal."

"Good. Then it's all settled. I'll take you down to meet the owner right after lunch."

"Thank you kindly, sir."

Miguel nodded at the elderly gent, but then glanced over at his newfound friends. He couldn't help but wonder about their curious looks... nor shake the feeling that he was getting a whole lot more than a job at a sawmill.

CHAPTER 3

*A*raceli peered out of the office window for the third time. It would just be her luck that old man Winslet would get a crazy idea like some former soldier working for her father. It was no secret that the Arroyos had lost their land during the war. Considering the do-gooder that he was, Mr. Winslet had probably gotten it in his mind that he could help heal some old hurt by bringing together this solder and her family. It wasn't going to happen, though. She'd see to that! She had sacrificed the opportunity to paint just so she could warn her father. However, the office was empty when she arrived. That meant he was probably overseeing the men who worked for him—maybe even up some tree himself. She hated the idea of him doing such dangerous labor at his age, but he insisted that he had the energy of a man half his age. Besides, there weren't enough hands to go around. He needed to be there.

And *that* was why she was going to take matters into her own hands. She wouldn't bother her father with trivial nonsense like an unwelcomed soldier. Instead, she would simply tell Atherton that there was no room for the newcomer.

The clopping of horse hooves caught her attention and she glanced out the window again. Sure enough, the two men came riding up in Mr. Winslet's wagon with the stranger himself steering the thing.

Just like those American soldiers... always taking over.

Well, she would put an end to any possibility of it happening at the Arroyo Mill. Araceli rushed out into the main foyer and then abruptly stopped. Wouldn't it look suspicious if she was already waiting for the men? She hurried back to the office she shared with her father and paced a few steps before spotting a stack of old invoices she had forgotten to file away. She snatched them up and rushed over to the cabinet that held all the important documents. The bell above the door chimed just as she started slipping the papers into their proper places. She waited to hear footsteps on the floor and a familiar voice called out.

"Howdy do?" Atherton Winslet said as he appeared at the office entrance.

"Good afternoon, Mr. Winslet. To what do I owe the privilege of your company? Are you needing more beams to brace the mine?"

The old man's eyes twinkled and Araceli immediately realized the first mistake she made—not thinking past common pleasantries after she had overheard the man specifically suggest the soldier seek work from her father back when they were at the café. The elderly gent didn't let on, though. He only gave her one of his crooked grins and motioned beside him. The soldier from earlier appeared, looking a bit surprised to see her. He removed his hat to properly greet her.

"How do you do, ma'am? The name's Michael St. James."

Araceli gave him nothing more than a brief nod, ignoring

his look of continued surprise when she failed to introduce herself. Instead, she turned back to Winslet. "I'm sorry, Mr. Winslet, but if you came looking for my father then I'm afraid you've arrived too late. He left a message that he would be working on site today."

"Did the message say whereabouts he'd be working?"

Araceli pursed her lips together. Of course, her father had indicated where he would be working. After all the two of them had lost, they always kept one another informed as to where they would be in case an accident occurred. Well, almost always. There were a few excursions Araceli may have forgotten to mention. However, she kept them secret only because she knew how much her father would disapprove.

She didn't feel much inclined to sharing any of that with old man Winslet. At the same time, what excuse could she give for withholding information as to where her father was? And she wasn't a liar by any means.

"Yes," she said.

The man waited a moment and then gave her an expectant look. "And could you please tell us *where* that would be, Miss Arroyo?"

"Well, I can but I'd have to warn you that he wouldn't be much for visitors. He is very busy trying to meet a deadline."

"Then he would more than likely welcome us with glee," Atherton insisted. His face set with determination. Araceli inwardly sighed. There was no use trying to dissuade the man any longer. He was determined to speak with her father and Atherton Winslet was the sort to always get what he wanted in the end.

"He's about a mile downriver," she finally revealed.

"Very well. We'll ride out that way to speak with him."

Araceli watched as the men began to leave and was suddenly struck with an idea. If she was on site when they asked her father for employment, then maybe she could give him some kind of signal to warn him that this stranger was not to be trusted. She sped up to Winslet and his guest.

"Perhaps I should go with you," she offered. "To make the appropriate introductions."

"Then perhaps *we* should be properly introduced first." Miguel gave her a roguish smile and offered a hand. "I never did catch your name, Miss."

"Arroyo. Araceli Arroyo."

She reached out, intending the handshake to be nothing more than a brief courtesy. However, warmth radiated up her arm the moment he touched her, making her breath catch. His eyes widened at her response and she quickly pulled back, drawing her arm close to her body as if she'd been burned. A fleeting glimpse in her peripheral vision drew her attention to Mr. Winslet, who looked like the cat that got the last bit of milk. She wanted to inquire as to what was so humorous but knew better than to sass Mr. Winslet. Not only was he the town founder and her father's best customer, but he really was a dear old man. In fact, he even gifted her with a new set of paints when they first arrived in town and he learned she enjoyed painting. So, she only gave him a gracious smile.

"Always nice to see the younger folks getting along," he said with a nod. "Makes me glad to think I'll be leaving behind a nice legacy one day—a town full of blessings. On that note, we best be getting along. I still need to make a stop at one of the mines today—hopefully with a few new beams I am indeed in need of. I'm praying your father can spare a few to avoid any nasty accidents."

"Mr. Winslet, you know my father would never turn you away. I'm sure he can accommodate your needs."

"Glad to hear it," he said and led the party out to the wagon. He briefly addressed Miguel. "Mr. St. James, my back ain't what it used to be. Why don't you help the lady on up?"

"I can help myself, thank you very much."

Araceli made a show of grabbing up her skirts and hiking them up high enough to show her calves. She didn't care, though. She would show this soldier just how little she—or her father—were in need of help. She scrambled up into the seat only to realize that she probably should have sat in the back so Mr. Winslet could keep his company. She was about to offer that she climb back down when Miguel boarded beside her.

"Hope you don't mind. Mr. Winslet suggested I do the driving so I can get a better lay of the land."

She glanced back at the elderly gent already comfortable in the buckboard. What could she possibly say?

"Suit yourself," she mumbled.

Miguel snapped the reigns against the horses and rode according to Araceli's sparse directions, which alternated between pointing and her busy stares at everything and anything she could set her sights on. The caw of a bird flying above, the sound of the wind whipping through trees, the sway of the grass alongside the path...

"You seem a bit preoccupied. Anything wrong?"

Aside from keeping company with the enemy?

"No," she said, deciding to keep a civil tongue in her head. She might not have cared much for the man, but she knew better than to be ugly towards anyone who never personally caused her harm—especially if that individual was a friend of Atherton Winslet. "I'm sketching my next painting."

"Sketching? How so? You haven't got any paper or anything."

Araceli smirked a little. "Goes to show what you know about an artist's mind, Mr. Saint James. The work begins before the brush even touches the canvas."

"Interesting," he said. "And, please, call me Michael. Everyone else does."

She only gave him a curt nod and resumed her studies. He cleared his throat.

"So, um, how do you do it exactly?"

"How do I do what?"

"The sketching thing you mentioned. How is it that the work begins before using the brush?"

"Mostly, it's a matter of looking at the lines and committing them to memory. I study the way a thing is and then reimagine it when it's time to capture the image on paper or canvas." She looked around for a moment and then pointed. "See that cloud over there?"

"Yeah, I see it."

"How would you describe it?"

Miguel shrugged. "I don't know. Kind of fluffy and white, I guess."

"Except it's not just 'fluffy and white.' Is it?"

He squinted at the cloud for a moment and then returned his focus to the road. "No, I suppose it isn't."

"What would you say makes it different than, say, that cloud over there?" She pointed to yet another and awaited his assessment.

He shrugged. "It's kind of wispy at the end and trails off into another cloud following right beside it. The color is a tad different, too."

"Not bad. Maybe you'd make a good artist."

He smiled. "Never really thought about clouds like that before. Maybe you can teach me how to see the world differently."

For some inexplicable reason, the suggestion of them spending time together made her heart skip a beat. However, the use of the word *differently* reminded her of exactly how much disparity there was between them. She was the "suffering" artist—the one who had lost everything. His kind were the ones who took it all away from her. She refused to say as much, though. Instead, pointing in front of them.

"There, up ahead. That's where the team is working today."

Miguel turned down a path that had been carved out, leading into the woods. A short drive in revealed a team of six men chopping and sawing away at several trees.

"Papá!" Araceli called out. Her father waved when he saw them. Slinging the axe he worked over his shoulder, he said something incoherent to his group of men and pulled out a handkerchief. He dabbed at his forehead and neck as he made his way to where Araceli and their guests awaited.

"*Hija*, what brings you out this way?"

"Señor Winslet is in need of some beams for his mine and was hopeful you would provide them."

"Of course, Atherton." He reached out a hand and the men briefly shook. "It's always a pleasure doing business with you."

"Thank you kindly, Juan. Perhaps we can talk privately for a moment—about the arrangements for delivery as well as a couple of other things."

"Sure. Let's step over here."

"Papá—"

"I'll just need to borrow your father for a minute, dear." The elderly gent gave Araceli a kind smile. "Then I'll be on my way right quick, because I still need to get up to that mine. Make sure I'm taking care of my men."

"I'll only be a minute, Chel. Then you can speak to me about whatever you wish."

Araceli silently fumed, but knew it was no good to act contrary. Her father took his business very seriously, and rightly so. While he had a rather successful operation running, he had to work hard to maintain it. She quietly watched the two men walk off some ways, actively engaged in a private conversation.

"Chel, is it?"

Startled, she jumped when she heard the sound of the shortened name. There he stood—the soldier—smiling down at her. The grin made her stomach flop in a way she didn't appreciate at all. Why was he able to make her physically react in such ways? It was quite infuriating!

"That is a familiar name used only by *mi familia* and friends."

His smile grew even wider. "Well, I'm kind of new to town. So, I'm in need of some friends."

She stared at him for a heartbeat and then looked away, concentrating on where her father and Atherton Winslet stood talking, silently willing for them to return. He waited for her to respond, the silence between them growing thicker. He finally pressed on.

"My apologies if I'm stepping out of line here, Miss Arroyo, but I have to ask since you've seemed out of sorts ever since we met. To be truthful, since the first time I saw you at the café. Could you please tell me if I've done something to offend you?"

She spun back around, ready to give him the sort of tongue lashing her mother would have bestowed if still alive to see her daughter behave so rudely. However, the thought of her mother doing exactly that caused a rare moment of clarity. Perhaps she was wrong for treating this stranger so harshly for his past. Besides, what did she really know of him? It could very well be possible that he served little to no role at all in the war. What if he had been a doctor who never fired a shot... or little more than a messenger delivering updates? The expression in his eyes was almost pleading—as if he wanted nothing more than to simply make her acquaintance.

"Let me see your hands," she finally demanded.

Miguel was momentarily taken aback. "My hands?"

"Yes," she explained. "I wish to see what kind they are."

Confused, he hesitated briefly but then thrust them out with a bit of flair, wiggling his fingers around. "Ta-da! There are two of them—each with five fingers. I have all ten toes, too. Care to see those, too?"

The comment was laced with a speckling of both sarcasm and humor, which brought her some inexplicable relief. The man wasn't some "barber's clerk" like Caleb Strauss— conceited, overdressed, and thinking money could buy him everything. She had no intention spending time with a barrel border, but she didn't want some fancy dandy either. Not that she had any intention of having *any* man to begin with. However, the looks on the faces of her papá and Mr. Winslet told her this soldier-turned-cowboy was about to become a lumberjack. That meant they would be seeing plenty of one another.

Araceli grabbed hold of his hands and turned them over, revealing tough callouses on both palms. She looked up at him, her breath catching. The intensity in his eyes and some-thing else about them seemed so familiar. She couldn't quite place it, but...

"Our apologies if we're interrupting."

Araceli dropped the newcomer's hands as if they had just turned into hot irons, her face as heated as such fiery metal. She turned to her father and lifted her chin in defiance.

"Nothing of great importance. I was examining this would-be lumberman."

Juan Arroyo smiled gamely at his daughter. "Well, I hope he's met with your approval because he'll be starting right now if he's got a mind for it."

"I sure do," Miguel eagerly shook hands with the gentleman and introduced himself for the fourth time that day. If things continued going as they were, he could possibly know everyone in town by the end of the week. "Where do you want me, sir?"

"You'll be working with me. That way I can show you how we do things around here. Then you can come back with the rest of the men for *la cena*. If you enjoy Mexican food, then you must try my daughter's cooking. She sets a table as fine as her mother did, God rest her soul."

"That will be just fine, sir. Thank you."

"You're welcome," Señor Arroyo said and then turned to his daughter. "You can manage one more. *Sí?*"

Araceli bit back a groan and forced a smile. How could she disagree when her father had compared her cooking to that of her late mama's marvelous creations? She would rise to the occasion and make all the signature dishes her mother had taught her. "*Sí, papa.* I can do it. Although, it might be a little later than expected since I didn't ride out on Inesh."

"Inesh?" Miguel questioned.

"That is her horse," her father explained.

"What an interesting name."

"Yes," Araceli said. "Papá got him from an Indian man back when we first moved here. The animal was born early and he was sure the creature would not survive. He actually wanted to put it down! Thankfully, his wife said it would be a sin to kill it. She helped do our laundry when we first came. That's how she knew us and the fact that I wanted a horse of my own. She convinced her husband to give it to me and— when the creature survived—she suggested we give him a name to reflect the strength he obviously had. I thought it only proper that he have a name to reflect his origins."

"The story is as fascinating as the name you chose."

"Well, if you like horses maybe you can see him sometime," her father offered.

"And perhaps the woman who helped save his life."

Araceli gave her father a measured look, silently informing him that she was keen to his game. He was sorely mistaken if he thought there would ever be a chance of a match with this newfound lumberman.

Señor Arroyo only smiled. "I suppose anything is possible."

Miguel looked between the two. There was a noticeable change in the air. He wasn't quite sure why, but he had felt similar tensions before.

"Far be it for me to get between a father and daughter, but I sure would like to get to earning my keep. Where should I begin, Mr. Arroyo?"

"This way," the man motioned. When Miguel reached his side, Señor Arroyo slapped his back, his voice lowering. "Thanks for saving me."

Miguel chuckled, quieting as soon as he caught Araceli's indignant glare. He turned back to his new boss. "I don't think everyone is too pleased with the idea of me working here... or even being around for that matter."

"Don't worry. She'll come around."

It was the last bit Araceli heard as the two men walked off into the woods, leaving her to mull over her father's confident declaration.

"Would you care for a ride back, Miss Chel?"

Araceli spun around, only then remembering Mr. Winslet's presence. She had a good mind to ask the man why he had to go and suggest this man—who was surely the next best thing to a criminal—work for her father.

"I suppose I must accept since we are to make arrangements for your delivery."

"Oh, well, your father and I done talked about that. He did me right. I still wouldn't mind driving you back if you'd like. I know you're probably wanting to get supper on and all."

He was right, of course. She did need to get supper on. However, she didn't care much for him reminding her... or maybe it was that strange smile of his. It was like he knew something she didn't—like the meal she made was for more than just eating.

"Thank you all the same, but I think I'd prefer to walk."

"You sure? It's a good mile back."

"I've walked farther than that before."

"Alone?"

She patted her skirt to indicate that she was armed.

"I'm never alone."

CHAPTER 4

"*T*hat was some of the best eating I've had in a long time," Miguel said as he leaned back in his chair. "My compliments to the cook."

"Gracias," Araceli said.

"Amen," Bart Frister agreed. "It's the kind of meal that'll make a man settle!"

She gave him a smile she hoped wasn't too encouraging. Every now and then he picked up work for her father—usually whenever one of the other women in town weren't showing him the interest he desired and he thought he'd try again with her. She had told him several times that she wasn't interested, but the word "no" seemed to fall on deaf ears when it came to Bart. Thankfully, it was only a dinner she had to suffer and that was amongst a table full of other workers.

"As I've said before," Señor Arroyo said, "my daughter sets an impressive table. Now, I believe you men all know the routine—except you, Miguel. Where are you staying tonight?"

The other workers who had been invited to dinner began

to clear off their places—a rule she was grateful her father had stipulated long ago so that she wouldn't be stuck with a bucket full of dishes at the end of each night. However, she was less concerned about the dishes at the moment. Curiosity had gotten the better of her. She waited with bated breath to hear Miguel's response and then silently admonished herself for caring at all.

"Seems like a nice enough evening. I figured I'd unpack my bedroll and see how many stars I could count tonight."

"Nonsense. We've got plenty of room."

"Thank you, sir, but I couldn't possibly—"

"He's right, papa." Araceli looked appalled. "I mean, we don't even know him. He could be a criminal."

"Araceli!" Her father glowered at her. "A woman of your age knows better than to speak to our guests in such manner. Apologize at once."

A look of mortification crossed her features and Miguel couldn't help but feel sorry for her. "No, your daughter's quite right. Neither of you know anything about me aside from the fact that I'm an old friend of Pete's. So, who's to say that I'm not a criminal? I ain't but you only have my word for that."

"Which is good enough for us. That and the fact that you are Pete's friend and Mr. Winslet has taken a liking to you is good enough for me," Juan Arroyo continued. "I trust his judgement above all others. It has yet to fail us. So, my offer still stands if you're interested… and you should be. It may be summer, but sometimes there's still a chill in the night air coming down from the mountains. Besides, you can never tell with the Miwok. They're relatively friendly—all of us keeping to ourselves. However, there's been a time or two that a warrior has felt the need for settling a score."

"Settling a score?"

"You know, for their people being forced off the land. Not that I blame them any. I understand how they feel."

Miguel wondered what his host could have meant, but he wasn't about to pry. Besides, the bigger concern was if what he was hearing was true. If so, then sleeping outdoors might not be the best idea. Displeased or not, he wasn't about to risk his neck simply because the boss man's daughter didn't like the idea of him being around. Which was another thing...

What was her problem with him anyway?

He wasn't entirely sure why, but he was fixing to find out —even if it was against his better judgement. There was something beyond her beauty that demanded further investigation.

Wait. Beauty?

"Well, *hijo*? Have you made a decision?"

"I'd be much obliged. Thank you, Mr. Arroyo."

"I'm happy to help. Now if you'll excuse me, I'm sure my daughter can show you to your room while I see the other men out."

Señor Arroyo excused himself, looking pleased with himself as he left the room.

Miguel stood, collecting his plate as he saw the other men do. "Is your father always so generous?"

Araceli stood and began her own cleanup. "Unfortunately."

Miguel froze. "Listen. There's something I've been aiming to say. See, I think we may have gotten off on the wrong foot here. Now that won't do at all with me working for your father, because we'll be seeing an awful good bit of each other. Would be nice if we could at least be cordial when we do so. So, I apologize if I've offended you for some reason."

"I'll take that under consideration," Araceli flatly stated.

She briskly stalked out of the room. Miguel was quick to pursue.

"Is that all? Could you at least tell me what I've done... or is this simply how you treat all the men?"

"The other men aren't murderers."

Miguel nearly dropped the plate. He fumbled, catching it right before it hit the floor. He swallowed hard against the lump in his throat, but it didn't do anything to help rid him of the feeling that the ground beneath him was about to swallow him whole. How did this woman know about his troubles? Was there a "Wanted" poster he was unaware of, hanging in town somewhere? Suddenly hot around his shirt collar, he tugged at it. It did little to cool him off or settle his nerves.

"I swear to you, I'm innocent. I didn't kill nobody."

Araceli spun around, eyes full of condemnation. "Of course you would be a liar, too. I saw your hands."

"My hands? What does that have to do with anything?"

"They are rough—not soft like some politician's son who served only to further his career, or like a general's hands because he spent more time in his private railcar sipping brandy than he did firing a rifle. I don't know how many you killed, Mr. St. James, but the number isn't what matters. The fact remains that you helped murder my people."

She dropped her plate in the bucket of soapy water and then sped off, leaving a confused Miguel behind as he pieced together what she was saying.

"Wait a minute!" He dropped his own dish into the wash basin and pursued her. She was already up the stairs and entering a room. She almost succeeded at slamming the door shut, but he caught hold of the handle. "Now just you wait a cotton-picking minute."

"How dare you stand in my room. Get out!"

Miguel refused. "Not until you listen to what I have

to say."

She crossed her arms in front of her chest and glared. "Well, then? What have you to say for yourself?"

"How about the fact that I was in a war and doing as I was commanded to do? How about the fact that for as many men as I killed, I saved that many too? And in case you were wondering, it didn't give me no pleasure to do it anyway. A lot of men—on both sides—signed up for the war, and a bunch of them were right sorry they did once it was all over."

"That's more than a lot of others got." Araceli sniffed, her eyes threatening to spill tears. "Some of them never got a chance to be anything other than dead."

She pushed the door closed on Miguel, forcing him to back up until it snapped shut.

"You'll have to forgive her."

Miguel spun around as his host climbed the last stair.

"You see, she was not an only child. She had brothers—three of them. All were lost in battle."

"And they fought for Mexico?"

"They did."

"But why? I mean, is that where y'all were living?"

"No. My children were born there, as were their mother and I. However, we moved to New Mexico when they were little more than babies. The boys returned to fight more out of principle than for any other reason. Also, we were afraid that we would be without a *patria* if America won—stuck someplace between the two with no country to really call ours. So, they chose the one that reflected our culture. It was an easy decision to make when their cousins contacted them, begging for help."

Miguel mulled over the man's explanation. He oftentimes felt at a loss for having lost his parents—people he never even met. He couldn't imagine what it would be like to lose three, close family members.

"I'm very sorry for your loss, sir."

"Thank you, *hijo*. It's been several years, though. Not that it makes it any easier. I will always miss my sons. However, at least I still have my Chel. She, on the other hand, has no one but this daft old man to care for and, one day, I'll be gone and then she'll have no one at all." Silence grew between them for a moment. Señor Arroyo sighed deeply. "Well, come this way. I'll show you to your room."

"I hate to be a burden," Miguel said but did as requested.

"You're not being one," Señor Arroyo insisted. "If I didn't want you here, then you would have never received an invitation to begin with. I have a good feeling about you, though."

Something about the man's praise resonated deep within Miguel. He stood a little straighter. "Thank you, sir. I promise I'll work hard for you."

"I'm not worried about that. If today was any indication, then I'm sure you will." He walked past one door only to open another on the opposite side. "This will be your room. It is beside mine. I'm in the middle."

His host gave him a pointed look and Miguel bit back a smile. It was only natural for a father to be protective of his only child—especially when it was a beautiful daughter.

Again?

Miguel chastised himself once more for being attracted to her. She wasn't quite a hellcat, but she had already proven there was a grouchy side to her. Nope. He best just leave that alone.

"I understand, sir. You've got my word that I'm every bit a gentleman and will continue to act as such while under your roof."

"Good. Just remember, we're all gentlemen in this town," Señor Arroyo said and then began walking away, mumbling under his breath, "not saints."

"What was that?"

"Uh, nothing. Have a good night."

"Thank you, sir."

Miguel entered his room and closed the door, surveying his surroundings. They were meek and modest, but comfortable. A small nightstand with an oil lamp beside a solid oak bed; wondering what in the world the man could have meant by that last remark. If he didn't know better, Miguel could almost swear that had been an open invitation to pursue Araceli...

Not that he would, of course. Besides the fact that the woman held an obvious dislike for him, he had too many other things to worry about... like the law.

And the St. James gang.

Miguel could punch a no-good, low life over that one. It was the one thing that made him strongly consider changing his name back to his given "Christian" one. That would mean being a man he had learned to hate years ago. Really, how he ended up the leader of a gang when he wasn't a criminal to begin with was a question he would love answered... especially since he hadn't even known the man he was accused of murdering! In fact, the name of the town he stayed in was about the only thing the Wanted poster did get right.

The poster!

It was hidden in his sack, which he had conveniently forgotten in his pursuit to learn why the boss man's daughter disliked him so intensely. The sack was still sitting beside his spot at the table. The last thing he wanted was for someone to accidentally find it and go rummaging through his stuff. It wouldn't do at all for the good folk of Blessings to think he was a criminal before he even had a chance to clear his name.

Miguel sat down on the bed. It would be better to wait until everyone fell asleep before going down to search for it. He only hoped it would still be there.

CHAPTER 5

A sliver of moonlight gleamed through the living room windows, illuminating Araceli's steps... and the rest of her, too.

Miguel had just approached the table when he heard footsteps. Ducking out of sight, he peered around the wall into the foyer, shocked to see her slip out the front door and quietly close it.

Where could she be going at such an hour?

He slung the sack over his shoulder and walked over to the window, looking out just in time to see her disappear around the house.

And out of his view.

He didn't want to admit to himself why that bothered him so much, but it did.

Fool girl. Who knows what kind of trouble she'll run into?

Hadn't her father said that he expected nothing less than gentlemanly behavior? Well, what kind of gentleman would allow a young woman to wander around, alone at night?

Miguel quietly popped open the door and slid out. With the door secured again, he walked in the same direction he had seen Araceli head a minute earlier and rounded the house, walking along it until he was in the back. A dim light glowed from the barn. He approached slowly, coming to a full halt when he saw the image in the corner. In this light, he could see everything clearly now.

There she stood—the woman of his dreams. Rather, the woman of his memories. It was like a vision reborn in the dusting of light. Once again wearing trousers, her hair pulled back into braids piled on top of her head, she stood in front of an easel with a jar of paint in one hand and a brush in the other. Her hand moved with such long, languid strokes that he almost felt envious of the canvas she lightly grazed.

Would she recognize him, too?

He tugged at his beard. Probably not. Shoo, he had known there was *something* familiar about her and couldn't quite put a name to it until only now—and she hadn't changed nearly as much as he had in the past—what had it been? A little more than four years, if he recalled correctly. Still, he remembered it so well. The way she had bravely risked her very innocence to claim what she was obviously most passionate about.

He wanted a better view, but didn't necessarily want her knowing he was there. He moved towards the stalls, thinking he could stand beside them and still stay out of sight. However, he had taken no more than two steps when he stepped on a rake and tripped. He fell forward, smacking his head against the stall door.

"Great goodness alive!" Miguel howled and slapped a hand to his forehead.

"Serves you right," Araceli said. "That's what you get for sneaking up on people."

"I wasn't sneaking," Miguel countered. The look on her face told him she wasn't convinced. "Oh, alright. Maybe I

49

was just a little. That's only because I saw you leave out the house."

"And you decided to follow me? Sounds awfully nosey."

"Well, it's late out… and… and… Well, look at how you're dressed! You shouldn't be roaming around like that. No telling what might get in someone's head."

"You mean someone like you?"

"No! I mean someone else—like maybe that Bart fella who was at dinner tonight."

Araceli snickered.

"What's so funny?"

"Oh, nothing, except the fact that I'm standing on my own property in one of the quietest towns this side of El Dorado County… and let's not forget that Bart went home quite some time ago."

"It still don't mean a thing. This here's a growing town with the promise of gold. You never know who might ride in. Bottom line, this place is too dangerous for a face like yours."

Araceli eyes grew wide. "I feel as if I've heard those words before."

Miguel cleared his throat, concerned that he had divulged too much and determined not to reveal anymore. "What I meant to say is that it's too dangerous to go wandering about at night. You never know what trouble you might run into—especially while alone."

Araceli lifted a challenging brow.

"As I've told others before, I'm never alone." She reached into the sack she had brought with her and pulled out a long six shooter. "There's a lot more than paints in my purse."

Miguel cracked a smile. Not only was she pretty, she was spunky too.

He liked that.

"That looks like a lot of gun for a little lady."

"I can handle myself—and the gun—just fine." She lifted it

and aimed at a beam, taking a pretend shot at it. She quickly lowered it.

"I think I'd like to see that." He crossed his arms and waited expectantly. "For you to hit that beam."

"What? Right now?"

"Sure. Why not?"

"My father would surely wake!"

"If you think he'd be upset to hear you shooting in the middle of the night, you could just imagine how he'd feel if he were to awake and find you missing."

"What do you care anyway?"

She was right. He shouldn't have cared.

But he did.

"Look. I'm new here and I've got an employer to impress. The last thing I'd want is for something to happen to you and for me to somehow be blamed. So, answer me at least this much. Do you know how to shoot that thing? I mean, *really* know how to shoot it… or is it more for show?"

Araceli squared her shoulders, her expression indignant. She looked ready to shoot off something alright—her mouth. However, she held back.

"I suppose I could work on my aim a little." She glared at him. "How did you know anyway?"

"First, because of the way you held the gun. It wavered too much—probably because it's a bit on the heavy side and you aren't used to shooting it. Second, your father doesn't seem the sort to be teaching his daughter to learn how to shoot. Am I right?"

"Maybe a little." Araceli shrugged. "So, what? Are you saying you're willing to teach me to shoot?"

He hadn't actually thought of that and wasn't entirely sure it was a good idea. How would her father react to find out he was teaching her how to shoot? At the same time, maybe it wasn't a *bad* thing either. It could be a good idea to get to know one another a little more. That might make things a little easier for the both of them while he was employed by her father. Besides, *everyone* needed to know how to protect themselves—especially a young woman with the habit of roaming around at night.

"You know what? I'll do it. I'll teach you how to shoot. Here's the deal, though. For every shot you miss, you've got to say something nice to me."

Araceli laughed. "If that isn't the saddest attempt I've ever heard for trying to get a compliment, then I don't know what is."

"What? Are you afraid you couldn't do it? You couldn't find even one nice thing to say to me?"

Araceli squared her shoulders. A grin stretched across her face. "Mr. St. James, I won't *have* to say anything nice to you. I'm not going to miss a single shot."

Miguel matched her smile, chuckling under his breath. "Then I guess you've got nothing to fear. Just name the time and place and I'll be there."

"How about tomorrow? During the *siesta?*"

"Siesta?"

"What? You don't know what a siesta is?"

"Yeah, I know. It's when you take an extra-long lunch so you can nap like a newborn. You folks do that around here?"

"My father is from another place and time. So, yes. He likes to rest for a while in the afternoon, which is why you all worked—and ate—later today than most normally would have."

"I was wondering about that. Except I didn't see anyone take a nap."

"Of course not. He was too busy showing you around—introducing you to the other workers, the mill, explaining jobs he has lined up. Your arrival meant more work."

He eyed her for a moment. She spoke matter-of-fact, but

with a tone to her voice that equaled her cool manner. He nodded assuredly. "Don't you worry none. I'll make up for any time lost in the job that I do for your father. In the meantime, we've got our own dealings to sort through. Do we have an accord? One kind word for each missed shot."

"And if I don't miss? What will you do for me?"

"Anything you want. Just name it."

"Anything at all?"

"That's right. You name it and I'll do it. You've got my word on that."

Her expression changed to that of a challenging one that was sure of winning. "Then you best pack your bags, señor, because you'll be leaving on the next coach out."

Miguel sized her up for a moment, measuring her words against her stand. He finally thrusted a hand out and they shook.

"You've got yourself a deal, Ms. Arroyo."

CHAPTER 6

They had found themselves a nice little clearing in the middle of the forest—a spot Araceli's father and his crew had previously worked. It was far enough out to be secluded so that no one would know she was learning to shoot, but close enough to hear the sawmill whistle. Miguel took the last bite of the packed lunch she had brought them and stood.

"Alright, you've got that thing loaded?" he nodded at the gun sitting on the blanket beside her.

"You've got your bags packed?" she countered and pulled herself up off the ground.

Miguel let out a hoot. "You're a real spitfire, Araceli. You know that?"

She ignored his comment about her personality, focusing instead on his way of informally addressing her. "I didn't know we were on a first name basis."

"Why wouldn't we be? We jumped past the niceties when I agreed to teach you how to kill a man like vermin."

"You're not going to teach me anything, sir. You'll see."

"Alright then, Ms. Arroyo." He addressed her formally, but

there was a slight tone of jest to his voice. "Let's see what you've got. Go ahead and shoot."

She lifted her gun, a mumbled prayer on her full lips, and aimed for one of the cans he had lined up for target practice. She squinted one eye to narrow her focus, the gun still wavering a bit in her hand. She pulled the trigger and the gun popped, her arm flinging above her head.

A chuckle escaped Miguel and she quickly turned to glare at him.

"Think you can do any better?" One hand rested on her hip. She cocked her head to the side and saucily said, "Oh, wait. You were a soldier. I'm sure you got plenty of target practice."

"Ouch. And after such an enjoyable afternoon filled with some of the best taquitos a man could possibly hope to find in this town. Really, that comment wasn't very nice, Ms. Arroyo… which isn't part of our deal. Remember?"

Her hand slid of her hip. She stood up a little straighter. Far be it for anyone to accuse her of squelching on a deal she shook on—especially if a compliment to her cooking was attached to it. "My apologies. What I meant to say is that you are obviously far more knowledgeable than I when it comes to this. I await your instruction."

She turned, mumbling something more under her breath.

"I'm sorry. What was that?"

Araceli gave him an innocent smile. "Oh, nothing. Whenever you're ready."

Miguel shook his head. He knew exactly what she had said about shooting *him* if she ever needed to. He wasn't even remotely worried, though. Her bark was obviously worse than her bite. Aside from the fact that he knew how to defend himself plenty, he didn't have any intention of ever giving her a reason to strike out against him—which was the motive to deciding to remain completely silent regarding their past in El Salvado. What she knew would hurt the both of them… and that was the last thing he wanted. Besides, how important was it really? A short conversation that lasted less than a couple of minutes was all it really amounted to.

Right?

"Well?" She gave him a quizzical look. "Are you going to teach me or not?"

Miguel shook off the fact that he had once again disappeared somewhere inside his troubled mind and quickly withdrew his own pistol, aiming at one of the cans. "Look, here. This is the proper way you hold a gun. Then you aim and… *fire!*"

His gun went off, perfectly hitting its mark. The can bounced off the post and twirled in the air. It landed on the ground and rolled across the grass.

"Alright. My turn." She quickly lifted her gun and shot, once again missing.

"Don't be in such a sure-fire hurry," Miguel advised.

He walked over, positioning himself right behind her. The heat off his body made the summer day feel even warmer than what it would have normally been. It became scorching hot when he wrapped his muscular arms around her, gently lifting her hands to aim at the cans. His slow, steady breath against the side of her ear made her face flush and her heart race.

"Try now," he said in a tone so low that it vibrated all the way down to her knees and back up to her elbows, making her legs and arms feel too weak to actually work. She commanded herself to focus and took the shot, still missing the can but doing much better as the bullet lodged itself into the post right beside it.

"That's not half bad," Miguel said. "Although, I think that now makes *two* compliments you owe me."

She looked over at him, their faces mere inches apart. His

shaggy sandy hair hung low, making his hazel eyes look even more intense. They drew her unknowingly closer towards him. He leaned towards her in response—the biggest mistake he could have made.

"What are you doing?" Her eyes narrowed and she straightened back up.

"Uh," Miguel ran a hand through his hair. "Nothing. I was just teaching you how to shoot."

Araceli lifted the gun and pointed it at one of the cans, focusing her hands and eyes on the target the same way Miguel had shown her. She pulled the trigger and the can popped off the fence. "Looks like you are a good teacher after all."

Miguel smiled. "I'll take that compliment... and one more."

The sound of the sawmill whistle called out for the men to return to work. Araceli grinned at her instructor. "I guess I'll have to owe you one."

"I'll hold you to that, Ms. Arroyo."

"You might as well call me Chel," she said. Then she hurriedly added, "Everyone else does. Might seem strange if you were the only one who didn't."

"Thank you kindly, Ms. Chel. Would you like me to walk you back?"

"I think I'll stay and practice a little more."

"Alright then. Don't get too good while I'm gone."

"Afraid the pupil will outrank the teacher?" she playfully asked.

"Naw," he said. "But what other excuse would I get to stand near you?"

Araceli's slight gasp prompted him to throw his head back with laughter. He snatched up his hat and plopped it on his head. Then he turned around and headed back off towards the sawmill.

"That was awfully bold," she cried out.

Miguel spun around but continued to walk, backwards.

"Don't worry," he called back. "I've seen your paintings. You like bold!"

Surprise registered on her face and he laughed again, facing forward once more and rushing off to work. She continued to stand there in silence.

Most men were interested in her father's wallet like Caleb Strauss, who saw the mill as a lucrative investment. This was the first man to show real interest in her work... to actually see *her*. A delicious feeling crawled through her—almost as pleasant as the one that had overtaken her during their shooting practice. She almost felt like running, or dancing or...

Painting.

Yes, that was it! She could paint the world anew, that's how inspired she felt. In fact, Araceli couldn't honestly recall the last time such enthusiasm claimed her. She pocketed her six shooter and then rushed over to where she had tossed her satchel upon first arrival, snatching it up. She would capture this moment forever, she determined, and plopped down on the ground in front of the shooting post. She pulled out a sketchbook and piece of charcoal. Her hands created short, jerky movements followed by longer ones as she quickly outlined the tin cans that remained on the post. Then she moved on to the ones on the ground beside the fence. The drawing was nothing fancy—quick and crude in her mind's eye, but sufficient until she could get home and flesh it out some more.

Home.

Araceli looked around and sighed. That would be quite a walk. Well, she had no one to blame but herself. Hadn't she been the one to suggest that he teach her to shoot to begin with? Knowing where the cleared sites were, she was also the one to choose where the lesson was held. Well, at least she had one consolation. She had learned to shoot. At least, she was fairly certain she had learned. She stood, the pistol slapping softly against her leg in the hidden skirt pocket. Reaching in, she pulled it out once again and examined it. She aimed at the can and squinted her eye, and then lowered the pistol again. Between the shooting lesson and sketching, her hand had grown tired and crampy. She switched the gun into the other hand to flex her fingers on the tired one. She shook it out and then grabbed hold of the pistol and took aim once more, focusing on her target.

Eso es. Riiight ther—

A loud cry similar to a woman's shrill scream sounded from behind Araceli. She jumped, her finger slipping off the trigger as she whirled around. There, opposite the clearing, stood a mountain lion. Tail swishing back and forth, it crouched low, strong muscles flexing. It slowly padded out of the brush towards her, large paws mauling the grass beneath it.

"Nice, kitty. Nice..." She gradually backed away from the advancing cat. The beast let out another shriek Araceli raised the gun and, closing her eyes, fired. The animal's cry forced her eyes open again. She didn't know where the bullet had gone, but it obviously hadn't hit the creature snarling at her. If anything, it had only made it angrier. Aware that she had only one bullet left in the chamber, she took aim again, this time much more careful than the last.

POP!

The bullet lodged into the ground right in front of the large cat, dirt spraying up in its face. The animal took a step back and gave Araceli a look that she could have almost sworn was one of irritation or even disgust. Whatever it was didn't matter, though. The cat twisted away and as easily as it had appeared, it disappeared back into the forest.

Araceli stood, breathless, and stared at the spot where the animal had been. She wasn't sure what exactly had happened —how she had survived—but she wasn't waiting around to find answers. Who knew if the mountain lion would decide she wasn't much of a threat after all and return. Gun now empty, she wouldn't be much of a threat at all if it did resurface. She turned and jetted across the clearing, into the trees and shrubbery that brought her closer to the safety of the sawmill. It was only once she cleared them that she felt like she could breathe again.

It was also then that she realized she had left behind her satchel of drawing supplies.

"Por toda la mala suerte!"

Of all the bad luck in the world, of course the worst of it would fall on her. She let out a small growl, but there was no going back. She would have to find a way to return later.

With more bullets.

She slipped the pistol back into her skirt pocket and headed straight down the path until the all the magnificence of the large mill came into view, looming on the horizon. Along with it, men running around it—much more so than usual. She got closer and their yells finally reached her ears. There was something wrong. She picked up the pace, gathering her skirts and breaking out into a swift stride.

"Auxilio!" one of their workers called out.

The cry for help forced her into a break-neck speed. She raced up to the building and into the mill door. A group of men scrambled about, forming a circle that blocked her vision. She bounced from one foot to the other, standing on the tips of her toes in an attempt to see over the crowd. When that failed, she finally began pushing through them.

"Con permiso... excuse me."

She broke through the throng of men to find both her father and Miguel laying on the ground. Her father moaned, clutching a hand to his forehead where a deep gash oozed thick blood. Miguel was beside him, a heavy log pinning down his legs.

"What happened?" she screamed, but the men ignored her as they went about helping the injured men. Again, she demanded, "*Qué paso?*"

"One of the logs broke loose while we were decking it. Rolled right over and almost onto your father, but Michael dove in and knocked him out of the way."

Men grabbed hold of the log. One counted off, "1, 2, 3..." and the trunk was hoisted up. Two of his co-workers pulled Miguel out while others helped Señor Arroyo stand.

"I'm alright. Get Michael a wagon and someone fetch Doc Edwards," he commanded. He stumbled over to the young man who had dove into danger for him. He knelt beside him. "Are you alright?"

"Yeah, I think I'll be fine. Just mangled up my legs a bit."

"Can you move them?"

He tried and let out a groan. "Hurts too much."

"Well, at least you've got feeling in them. That's something." Señor Arroyo helped him sit up a bit and embraced him. "Thank you, *hijo*. You saved my life."

A hard knot formed in Araceli's throat. She swallowed hard against it. The image of the two men together reminded her of a time when her brothers were still alive. The look on her father's face was all she needed to know. A former soldier or not, her father *needed* someone like him.

Maybe she did, too.

A man pushed through the crowd that had formed once again. "Señor Arroyo, we've got the wagon."

A group of men gathered around Miguel and lifted him up into the back of a buckboard.

"And the doctor?" His boss asked.

"Raul went for him. He'll bring him to the house."

"Good man. Thank you." Her father turned to her then. "Go back to the house and prepare anything you think Doc Edwards will need. Then make a nice strong broth for Michael."

"*Sí, papa.*"

Araceli sped off to do her father's bidding, her heart racing as fast as her feet. Worry ebbed through her. Would Michael be alright? What if his legs had been broken—or worse? The logs the men hauled were extremely heavy, and the work was known to carry its own set of dangers. What if Michael's legs had been so badly mangled that the doctor couldn't save them?

And why did she suddenly care so much?

She knew the answer and was surprised that it didn't bother her. In fact, the only thing that was of concern at the moment was what all Doctor Edwards was going to need to do his job correctly. She was thankful that the house and mill were situated so close to one another. It made it easier for her to return home and do as her father requested.

She made it to the front door before the men and set to work, starting a fire and gathering clean cloths. She had just made her way up the stairs to enter the guest room and turn down the bedsheets when she heard the front door open. She stopped at the top of the stairs.

"This way," she called down to them.

They quickly made their way behind her, their patient grunting in pain, and laid him in the bed.

"I don't want to make you even more uncomfortable than you already are," she said, "but I think we should cut away these pants before the doctor arrives."

He gave her a wayward smile. "I ain't shy."

"Neither am I," she replied ruefully and fetched a pair of scissors. Then she returned and set to work, finishing just as the doctor arrived.

"Good work," the doctor commended her. "I'll take it from here."

She nodded hesitantly, but then made her way to leave. She closed the door to allow them some privacy.

"How is he?" her father, surrounded by some of his men, called from the bottom of the stairs.

Araceli opened her mouth to speak, but nothing came out. Suddenly overwhelmed, she spun on her heels and headed straight to her room—the only private sanctuary that would allow her the opportunity for a good cry.

CHAPTER 7

*M*uffled voices were followed by shadowy figures. Why did Miguel feel like his head had been pounded on by a few dozen men?

"My head hurts," he mumbled.

"It's the medicine," a familiar voice explained. "The doctor gave you some laudanum for the pain, and said that we're to give you another dose should it become unbearable, but no more than six doses in a day."

"How many have I had today?"

"None."

"None? But you just said—"

"I know, but that was two days ago. You've been asleep ever since."

"Two days?" Miguel rubbed at his blurry eyes until things came into focus. Araceli stood at his bedside. "Why'd you let me sleep so long?"

"We figured you needed the rest after everything you had been through."

He tried to sit up. "And what exactly have I been through? What did the doctor say?"

"That you're very fortunate. There were no breaks, but your legs are still fairly mangled. They were bruised and swollen clear up to your—"

His eyes grew wide. "How would you know what they look like?"

"I don't. I'm just quoting the doctor," she admitted. A sly look crossed her face. "Although, I could have sworn a certain someone said he wasn't shy about such things."

"I'm not," Miguel countered. "It's just that no man wants a woman seeing him at his worst."

"I don't think it was your worst," Araceli offered. She sat down on the bed beside him and gingerly reached out, taking his hand in hers. "In fact, I think you were at your best. My father told me what happened. The other men confirmed his story, too. His not quite in peak form anymore. With his age and physical condition, he probably would have died had that log hit him. Michael, I don't think I can thank you enough. You saved him. You saved me, too."

"I did?"

She nodded. "Yes. That day in the woods when you taught me how to shoot? Well, a cougar came shortly after you left."

"What?" Her words startled Miguel, forcing him into nearly sitting upright. He groaned.

"*Cuídate!* You'll hurt yourself again if you're not careful. Sit up slowly."

Miguel did as instructed and she quickly snatched up extra blankets she had brought in earlier, placing them behind his head to keep him supported.

"Would you like some more of the laudanum?" she asked.

"Actually, I would prefer something to eat if you've got anything. Then I think I'd like to hear exactly what happened."

"Of course," she said and excused herself from the room. She returned several minutes later, carrying a tray. "I've been making *caldo de pollo* each day—in case for whenever you awoke. I know some people would not want to eat a hot dish like this on such hot summer days, but my mother always said it was a healing dish."

"I don't mind at all," Miguel smiled. "I love chicken soup."

"Then you'll really love this recipe. It's one of my special—"

She fell silent.

"What's the matter?" he asked.

A strange look passed over her face. "How did you know it was chicken soup? I told you what I made in Spanish."

"I... um... I guess I picked it up along the way."

"Oh, yes. I suppose that would make sense... with the war and all."

Part of him wanted to tell her she was wrong and that he had picked up the language from the field hands he worked with on his grandfather's farm—people like his aunt who, after posing some inexplicable threat to her grandparents, were released from their jobs. He couldn't tell her that, though. He couldn't admit that half of him was just like her. Then she would *never* understand why he had fought for the American side. Heck! He wasn't so sure he understood it himself anymore.

He cleared his throat. "It does smell mighty good. Probably tastes as good as your paintings look."

She set the tray down on the table beside his bed. "I'm sure it tastes much better than my paintings look—especially the latest ones."

"Why's that?" he asked right before she stuck a spoonful of food in his face. He smiled. "You're going to feed me?"

"If you ever stop talking."

He chuckled. "Alright. I promise to keep my mouth closed. Well, except for when I open wide for another mouthful. You go on and tell me about that cougar in the woods."

She did as requested, retelling the same story she had shared with her friend, Maxine, when the woman stopped by to call earlier that morning.

"You didn't hit it?" Miguel tried to holler around the food in his mouth. He swallowed. "You're lucky to be alive!"

"My friend said the same thing." Araceli lifted the spoon once more, but he waved it away. She set the bowl back down on the table. "Maxine couldn't believe that I was able to scare it off like that, because I didn't actually hit the animal and cause any pain for it to connect with fear. Why should it have been afraid of me? Yet, I believe it truly was. At the very least, it was wary of me—as if it knew I *could* harm it."

"Well, at least you know to stay away from that area now."

"Stay away? I can't do that."

"Why on earth not?"

"I have to go back. I left some of my supplies there."

"Those supplies aren't worth your life, Chel."

"Those supplies help me *live* my life."

"Can't you just get more?"

"That's easy for you to say." she popped up off his bedside and strode out of the room only to return a minute later, several jars of paint in her hands. "See these? They're all I have left to paint with... and it's not like they come from your general mercantile."

"Where did you get them?"

"I made some of them." She quickly held a hand up. "Before you suggest I simply make more, hear me out. The ones that I made myself were from flowers I can't readily find or buy around here. For example, I have one color that comes from the thread tip of a saffron flower. It came in my possession while I was in El Salvado thanks to an old friend named Georgia. I don't know where she got the seeds for her garden, but it seemed like she had some sort of magic touch —anything she wanted, she found, and anything she planted, grew. One of those things was saffron. This is a problem, because now I'm not able to paint the Cempasuchil flower the right color."

"But if you could get your hands on the flower, or even the seeds, then you could make more of the paint?"

"Yes."

"Then all we have to do is wait until we can write your friend to send some to you."

"And risk the plants being destroyed or lost by some careless driver?"

"Alright. We'll take a visit to El Salvado ourselves."

The words were out of his mouth before he even had a chance to think about what he was saying. El Salvado? That would be a terrible idea! That's where the law was after him the most, because that's where the murder had occurred. He could never go back.

Araceli gave him a curious look. "You'll jump in front of a falling log to save my father, but won't brave the forest once more?"

"That's different," he insisted. "Your father's life was at risk."

"I am at risk of losing my supplies."

He sighed. It wasn't quite the same, but he relented anyway. "Fine. I'll go and get them as soon as my legs are healed up."

She gave him a generous smile. "That's very kind of you, but your legs could take weeks to heal. I don't think it's a good idea if I leave them out there that long. Too many things can happen between now and then. What if it rains?"

He reached out and took hold of her hand, his eyes filled with serious concern. "Please, don't go back there alone."

The warmth of his hand engulfed hers, traveling up to her

arm and scrambling her thoughts. "You talk too much," she mumbled.

A sly smile crossed his handsome face. "I can do more than talk."

The suggestive comment made her head swim even more. She shook her head in a desperate attempt to clear her mind. "Perhaps we shouldn't speak at all."

"Kind of strange to sit here in silence. Don't you think?"

He looked at her in a way that made her shiver on the inside. It was a foreign feeling to experience on such a warm day. She moved towards a canvas she had set up the day before. "I have some work to finish anyway."

"I noticed that. Are you painting my pain?"

She gave him a rueful smile. "Actually, it has nothing to do with you. My subject of interest happens to be the Cempasuchil flower."

"Hmm. That sounds intriguing."

"Oh, don't pretend you're interested. Men don't like such silly things."

"That's not true. I enjoy hearing about anything that interest you—like that flower you just mentioned. It might be nice to see something like that one day."

She was slightly flattered by the thought that he liked hearing about things that appealed solely to her—especially when those things coincided with her painting. Most of the prospective beaus she had known before cared little to none that she was an artist. Plus, he had taught her how to shoot— in secret no less. She could appreciate the fact that he saw past her father and his business to acknowledge her personal needs and desires.

"You would like to see such a flower?" she finally asked.

"I sure would."

Araceli put the brush down and swiveled in her chair until she faced him. She appeared quite pleased. "Well, the painting isn't finished. But perhaps you would like to hear the legend of how it came to exist in the meantime."

"Dinner and a bedtime story? Count me in."

Araceli chuckled and picked up the brush, her voice matching the strokes along the canvas. "Once upon a time—a long time ago, when my people were still Aztecs—there was a young girl named Xóchitl. Beside her lived a neighbor boy, Huitzilin. The boy loved to run off and have adventures, and even though it was unusual, the girl's parents allowed her to go off with him. Together, the two of them would have great explorations. They would come home every evening with interesting forest finds—a spearhead or frog, or whatever it is children believe to be great discoveries." Araceli's hand paused over the painting. "Am I boring you with my story? I can stop if you wish."

Miguel sat up a little straighter. "Not at all. Please continue."

She gave him a satisfied smile and turned back to the canvas. "So, they spent their entire childhood together and became the best of friends. Of course, the only natural thing happened—the thing that is bound to happen when two people spend so much time together."

She fell silent.

"Go on," he encouraged. "What happens when two people spend that much time together."

She shrugged, refusing to admit that her face had grown warm again. "They fell in love, of course."

"And they lived happily ever after?"

"Of course not. Leave it to a man to rush right ahead," Araceli scoffed. "Do you not know anything about the Aztecs at all? The conquistadors came, declaring war. Hitzilin was killed in battle. So they did not live, as you say, 'happily ever after.' Everyone always dies in the end."

She turned back to her painting, her nose held half an inch higher than before.

"You call that a story? Why, you might be a talented artist, but you're a terrible storyteller!"

"Oh? Do you think you could do better?"

Miguel laced his fingers together and settled a little further into the pillow. "As a matter of fact, I do. Once upon a time, there were these two Aztecan youngins like you done mentioned. I mean, these two were so in love, they was beside themselves. Xóchitl spoke all nice to the boy and only made eyes at him. So, he done the same for her and even took her up to this big hillside where they could offer up flowers to the sun god, Tonatiuh. Well, just like it'd always done before and is bound to happen again, sure enough war broke out... and you're right. Hitzilin was taken up to glory during one of the battles. Word got back to Xóchitl and she was just devastated! I mean, she done gave her whole life to this boy already—letting him stick frogs in her face and whatnot."

"Oh, stop it! That's not how it goes."

"It sure does. They couldn't get along a hundred percent *all* the time. It ain't natural. Now you want me to finish this story or not? Cause I can stop if you wish."

She squinted at his canny ability to turn her words around, but smiled her approval, nodding that he should continue with his version of the legend.

"Very well. Like I was saying, poor boy went to glory and she was a mess over losing him. So, she went to the sun god and begged him to turn her into a flower. Well, this is the part that gets a little muddy. See, some say that she had been such a faithful follower that Tonatiuh rewarded her by doing just that. Me, on the other hand, I think he was tired of her murdering all them flowers and thought it was the best way to make her stop picking them."

Araceli laughed. "You're silly."

A wild grin stretched across Miguel's face. "Hope you don't mind me saying so, but that's a mighty fine laugh you've got right there."

The compliment caught her off guard and set her heart fluttering once more. The way he kept making her insides react was unnerving. Her grin slightly diminished.

Miguel feared he might have been laying it on too thick, being too flattering too soon. He rushed on, " Anyway. She became a flower and they did live happily ever after, because Hitzilin had been turned into a hummingbird. So, anytime you see one of them sweep down low to drink from one, that's really him... giving his gal a kiss."

"Is that so?" Araceli asked, her voice soft and mesmerizing.

"Yes, ma'am."

Her smile was so sweet and tender that it almost made him want to channel Hitzilin in hummingbird form and soar right off the bed to claim Araceli for himself. That could be disastrous, though. They weren't quite there yet... and probably wouldn't be for some time, if ever. After all, he had the law on him from New Mexico. Even if that mess wasn't a roadblock between the two of them, there was still the issue of his past. She deserved to know who he really was. He simply couldn't bring himself to tell her, though.

"I must admit, Michael, I was a little startled by your story."

Miguel snapped out of his thoughts. "How so?"

"Your version of the Cempasuchil's origin was funnier than I've heard it told before, and I thoroughly enjoyed it. What caught me off guard, though, was the fact that you knew the end."

"You mean I was right?"

"Please don't feign ignorance." Araceli gave him a pointed look. "How did you learn of the legend?"

"I've been around. You know that, though."

The expression on her face said that she wasn't entirely convinced by his explanation. Much to his chagrin, silence settled over them—which wouldn't do at all. They were getting on with each other so nicely. It would be a shame for things to end on such a sour note. He struggled to find something to say, blurting out the first thing that came to mind.

"I wish I knew how to paint."

The declaration caught her off guard.

"You do?"

Miguel bit his tongue. That had been an unexpected response! Oh, well. What could be the harm in learning how to paint? He shrugged. "Uh, yeah. Why wouldn't I want to?"

Araceli looked thoughtful. "That might not be such a bad idea. It's not like you have anything better to do. You certainly won't be hauling logs anytime soon. The accident put you out of work for at least another week—maybe even two—and the accounts I have at the mill aren't so pressing. I suppose I could teach you a thing or two if you really are interested."

Miguel liked the idea of them spending time together. Araceli wasn't like other women he had known before. Of course, he realized that the first time they met. That was the only reason he could think that he never truly forgot about her.

"So, when do we start?" he finally asked.

"Tomorrow. Of course, we haven't discussed payment yet."

"Payment? I didn't make you pay."

"Oh, yes, you did. I had to give you a compliment for every missed shot. Remember?"

Miguel chuckled. "I see. You're wanting me to pay you compliments."

"Not at all."

His face screwed up with confusion. "Then what is the payment?"

"That you answer whatever question I ask."

"Uh," Miguel hesitated. "What kind of questions?"

"That's for me to know and you to find out." Araceli placed the brush down and held a hand out. "So, what do you say?"

Miguel didn't like the idea of answering questions that revealed too much, and he certainly wasn't a liar. Well, not really. Going by the English version of his name didn't constitute as a lie in his book. So, he didn't want to start making up stories just to answer her questions now. Would he have to, though? It wasn't like she had completely stuck to their bargain for the shooting lessons—giving him wayward compliments and even holding back one.

He could do the same.

He grasped her outstretched hand. "I believe you've got yourself a deal."

CHAPTER 8

"*H*ow are you feeling, *hijo?*"

Miguel carefully tested his legs, shifting from one foot to the other. "The legs are still a little sore, but things seem to be in working order."

"Well, the doctor said that might happen. The important thing is that the swelling has gone down."

"Yes, that is important," Miguel agreed. He picked up his hat and placed it on his head. Then he walked over to the mirror to get a good look at himself. No number of hats, scarves or anything else could cover up his ugly mug. Two weeks of not even trimming and his beard looked like it was trying to give birth to a bird's nest. He tugged on it. "I think this is the longest I've ever seen this thing get."

"I was going to mention something about that," Señor Arroyo said. "I think a beard is much like a woman's hair. When it is properly cared for, it is like a crown—a thing of pride. However, it can also be something quite frightening when allowed to become unruly. No young woman around here—especially one like my daughter—is going to be overly excited about a beard like that. You understand, *no?*"

"Yeah, I think so. Although, I'm wondering why you believe Araceli would care about a thing like that... or me, for that matter."

Señor Arroyo smiled knowingly. "I am getting older, yes. However, I am well aware when a man and woman care for one another."

"That's right! I forgot about the ever-helpful Ms. Priya," Miguel teased.

The older gent cleared his throat. "Yes, well, let's not change the subject. I'm speaking about you and my daughter. I've passed this room plenty of times in the past couple of weeks and have seen the way you two look at one another. Do you deny your feelings for her?"

Miguel felt equal parts embarrassed and elated. It appeared he had an ally who supported the match. The only problem was that the man didn't know everything he should about Miguel.

"I don't deny them, but I don't think my feelings are altogether appropriate either."

"Why in the name of *Dios* wouldn't they be? What are your intentions with my daughter? Are they honorable?

"Of course, sir."

"Then what is the problem? You are both young... and I'm not going to live forever, either. I would like to see my daughter settled down, with the opportunity to find true happiness again—which I think has finally happened. I wouldn't mind meeting a grandchild or two, either, but that is for another discussion."

"I understand, sir." Miguel's nerves bundled up into a ball and his senses were on full alert. He noticed little things around him. There was a spot on the wall that looked much like one of Araceli's paints. Had it always been there? And the way the sunlight streamed through the window, casting light into the room. Had the sun always been this bright? He suddenly remembered he was still wearing his hat indoors. too. He swiped it off his head, mashing it in his hands until the brim was nearly beyond repair.

"Well, whatever it is can't be worth destroying a Stetson over. Get it out, *hijo*."

Miguel released a slow, pent up breath.

"I'm afraid I haven't been completely honest. You see, I know your daughter. I mean, I knew her. Rather, I've *met* her before. Once. Briefly. It was but for a few minutes, you see, and I... well, I..." Miguel quietly groaned. "I'm making a real mess out of this."

Juan Arroyo smiled. "You are speaking about El Salvado?"

Miguel's mouth dropped open with shock. He snapped it shut again. "How did you know that?"

The elderly man chuckled. "*Ay*, the young... they think they know so much. However, do you really think I would allow just anyone to stay in my house? *Claro que no*. Pete had told Mr. Atherton Winslet all about you before you even arrived.

"What? He wasn't supposed to tell anyone."

"Well, what did you think—he was going to keep it from the man who helped him more than anyone else? Atherton is like a fairy godfather or something—he makes everyone's lives better. That's exactly what he did for Pete. So, there are very few secrets between the two of them. When Atherton approached me and we walked off in the forest to speak, he told me all about you—your past service in the army and the Americanized name you used. So, I immediately contacted some friends in El Salvado. I learned about your attempts to buy my land."

"I'm sorry, sir. I never went through with it, though."

"I know you didn't."

"But how?"

Juan shrugged like a man in a poker match finally laying

his own hand on the table. "Because I sold it before it could be seized."

Miguel was staggered by the man's declaration. "You *sold* it? That's why they refused my offers!"

"Yes... but that doesn't quite explain how you knew my daughter in El Salvado."

"She showed up there one night. I caught her inside, collecting some old jars of paint."

Señor Arroyo sighed. "That does sound like my Chel. Now you understand why I am concerned. She takes some of the most dangerous risks, but it is not because she is ignorant or careless. It is only because she's so passionate for her work."

"She has every reason to be," Miguel confided. "I think she's probably the greatest artist I've ever known. The way she pays attention to the smallest details and how she mixes both light and shadows on the page... it expresses a real depth of emotion."

"I see my daughter has gotten to you—filled you with some of her zeal for experiencing life in a way so few truly understand or even appreciate."

"Very much so. More than I care to admit, I'm afraid. My life has been a bit... complicated."

"Yes, I know about the accusations you face regarding the murder of a bartender there. Your friend, Pete, has been quietly seeing to that matter."

"He has?"

"*Asi es.*"

It was a lot to take in at once—the fact that Juan Arroyo had always known who he was and that Miguel's name might be cleared without facing any real consequences. Now if only winning Araceli would be as simple.

As if the concern were painted on his face, Juan Arroyo advised him. "Perhaps if you would be as honest with my daughter as you have been with me, then things would not seem so impossible."

"You don't think it would be better if you spoke with her instead?"

"No. There are certain affairs a man must see to himself."

"Yes, I suppose that's true."

"Besides," Señor Arroyo continued, "there seems to be a problem down at the mill. The logs aren't flowing down the river the way they usually do."

"Probably a beaver built a dam further down, or maybe some other brush got caught up."

"That's what I was thinking, too. That's why I'll leave it to you to sort things out with *mi hija* while I go find the source of our production problem. I'll let you know what I find out when I return."

"Hopefully, you'll have some good news."

"*Espero que si...* let's pray we both do."

Miguel momentarily felt confident that Señor Arroyo was right as the old man assuredly strolled out of the room. He turned back and studied himself in the mirror, deciding Araceli's father was right. The scraggly mountain man staring back at him wasn't about to win over her heart. It was as plain as the beard on his face that he was in hiding —literally.

He ambled over towards his satchel and pulled out a razor that was still sharp only because it had never been used before. Then he returned to the mirror with it, the wash bowl and a bar of soap. He lathered up the soap and rubbed it into the beard until it was completely covered in suds. Then he brought the blade to his face and down again, removing a fair deal of his former self. He repeated the process, the smooth strokes somewhat reminding him of Araceli and the way she painted. This was his canvas, though. He would shape it just as artistically as she did hers with paints and charcoals.

Miguel carefully trimmed along the edges of his generous lips. Satisfied with the results, he set the razor down and washed the remaining soap of his face.

That's more like it.

He had to admit that even he was surprised by the man staring back at him. It was a man who could proudly present himself to a woman who could find the beauty in almost anything.

He just hoped she would be able to find it in him.

CHAPTER 9

"*S*o, tell me. What else is he like? Surely you've got more than that to share."

Araceli laughed at Maxine's enthusiasm. She continued perusing the current fabrics Edward Mosier offered in his mercantile. "I'm not sure what more you're looking for. Favorite color and foods and some places he's seen... I've told you most everything he's shared with me—everything I can remember leastways."

"But that's not what I want to know," Maxine insisted. "Not that there's anything wrong with all that, of course. I'm more interested in knowing how *you* feel about those things, though. What is he like to you?"

Excitement rose at the idea of how she personally felt about Michael, but she quickly squelched any thought that it meant more than a passing fancy. She shrugged. "Why should I feel anything at all?"

Her friend grasped her hand with a subdued squeal. Several matrons looked up from their own purchases to give them pointed stares. The two young women grew serious until the women walked away. Subdued snorts escaped with their laughter as they rushed off into the opposite direction. Maxine pulled Araceli into an empty aisle of sewing notions.

"I knew it! You like him."

Araceli wanted to deny it, but she didn't condone lies. "Oh, alright. Perhaps I'm slightly intrigued."

Her friend clapped. "Well, it's about time someone finally turned your head."

"Ha! You're a fine one to speak. When are you going to give Bart Frister a chance?"

"Absolutely never… and don't try to change the subject."

"Which was?"

"You and mister soldier boy." Maxine gasped at the reference she made. "I'm sorry, Araceli. I forgot. You don't mind, though, do you? I mean, you've gotten past that. Right?"

The past two weeks had seen too many restless nights as Araceli contended with the same question. Each day Michael healed was one more day for her to really examine how she felt about him. It was interesting how quickly she had adjusted to the idea of him once being a soldier who fought against her own people. It should have remained a sore subject for her. Instead, it faded into the background as if truly unimportant. She wasn't entirely sure if it was due to the fact that she was getting to know him better, or the feeling she couldn't shake that they were intimately connected. It reminded her of the story of Xóchitl and Huitzilin crossing all obstacles to remain together through the sands of time.

"To be honest, there are greater worries in life," she finally answered.

Her friend smiled approvingly. "I'm glad you're beginning to realize that."

They went up to the counter to pay for their purchases where the owner, Ed Mosier, sifted through a pile of newly arrived mail that his son had brought back along with other supplies on his monthly trip from Sacramento.

"Good afternoon, Mr. Mosier. Any good news?"

"Just the usual." The elderly gent's eyes worked over the mail. He handed a single sheet of paper to his son. "Would you hang this up outside, please?"

"Yes, sir."

The man disappeared outside while his father added up first Maxine's purchase and then Araceli's basket of goods. She handed over the money and bid the owner a good day.

"Well, I better get on home. Thank you for the afternoon tea," Maxine said.

"I enjoyed it. *Nos vemos.*"

"Wait! I know that one... Um... See you later?"

"*Eso es.*"

"I know what that means, too." Maxine held her head up a little higher. "Take care, *amiga.*"

The two women briefly embraced. Araceli stood on the steps of the storefront, watching her friend head off further into town. She glanced around the busy Main Street and noted the normality of people promenading down it, lost in their daily routines of competitive commerce with weighed down wagons kicking up dust. Filtered conversations drifted on the air. She turned the opposite direction to return home, halting when she noticed the paper Mr. Mosier's son had hung out front. She grabbed hold of it and snatched it down.

Wanted
Mike "The Saint" James
$500

BLOOD RUSHED to Araceli's head. Her pulsed raced uncontrollably—much like her horse, Inesh, when he was trying to prove himself to one of the mares.

It was Michael… but it wasn't. The beard was gone; the face a touch more slender and younger. It was a familiar one… a face she had briefly seen years ago, masked by shadows in her darkest memories of El Salvado and the hacienda they once owned.

She read the wanted poster several times, as if a new name or different image would suddenly appear.

"Everything alright, Ms. Chel?" Mr. Mosier called from behind.

Araceli quickly stuffed the paper into the bottom of her basket. She turned to the store owner, still standing in the doorway. "Yes, sir. Everything is fine."

"Are you sure? You look a little peaked."

She waved his concern away. "It's just this summer heat. I'm sure I'll be fine once I get out of it."

"Alright. You take care of yourself now, you hear?"

"Yes, sir. You have a blessed day."

"You, too, Ms. Chel."

Araceli secured her basket of goods to the back of Inesh's saddle. Then she took the rein in hand, hiked up her skirts and mounted him. She urged him into a steady walk, picking up the pace as she made her way to the end of Main Street, cutting down the path with choices veering off left, towards the mines, and right, to the sawmill. She rode past the men hard at work, barely nodding an acknowledgement as they lumbered around the yard, but noting that her father wasn't there. She hardly questioned why, though. Her mind was filled with too many thoughts and more emotions than she cared to admit. She knew this face on the poster. She remembered clearly now. How did she not recognize him before as the soldier from El Salvado? For weeks he had been right under her nose, parading around like some innocent pariah who came to town all down and out on his luck. Well, he most certainly was out of it now. He obviously thought her family was easy pickings—perhaps somehow learned of her father's success in California.

That's it!

They still kept in contact with friends and extended family in El Salvado. Someone must have mentioned all they accomplished in Blessings, and figured they would be easy pickings. Well, he had another thing coming if he believed that! She had every intention of settling the score with a man associated with those who had not only ran her family off their land, but murdered two of her brothers.

She would kill him.

No, she would allow her father that honor.

De veras, Araceli?

Truthfully, though. What foolish thoughts! Who was she trying to convince? She didn't have it in her to do something like that. Neither did her father.

Sure as the day was long on a summer of no rain, they could run him out of town, though. They could notify the proper authorities, too. In fact, Pete could take him in. He would do it even if the two of them were friends. She was sure of it. After all, the law was the law and this man was just as the poster stated—wanted for murder.

Araceli rode up to the house and was so angry hot that she abandoned both Inesh and her basket of goods, pausing only long enough to grab the poster out of the carrier. She strode up to the house, reached into her skirt, pulled out the six shooter and threw open the door, stepping inside with the gun raised at eye level. She should have saved the grand entrance, though. Despite knowing that her "charge" was once again ambulatory, he was nowhere to be found.

Bang!

She jumped at the sound of something clanging in the kitchen. She followed the noise, lowering the gun to her side to press against the wall and peer through the crack of the partially opened kitchen door. She wasn't able to see much, but it sounded like someone was cooking.

"*Ooow!*"

Miguel's howl sounded from the other side of the door, forcing Araceli out of her hiding spot. The man briefly waved a hand around in the air before sticking it in the bucket they used for drinking water.

"What are you doing?" she demanded.

He pulled his hand out of the bucket. "Uh, I *was* trying to cook. I forgot to use a towel before grabbing the skillet, though."

Araceli looked around the kitchen, evidence of his cooking skills everywhere. Half the place was a terrible mess with flour powdering the floor and sticky chicken parts dripping off the counter, vegetable scrapings stuck to them like feathers to tar. However, a delicious smell wafted through the air, and the table was set with a basket of freshly picked flowers.

"I know they aren't quite your favorite, but I couldn't find any Cempasuchil. I hope you'll like these enough not to shoot me."

He motioned and Araceli looked down to the gun she still gripped in her hand.

"I... I..." She was so overwhelmed that she didn't know what to say. "I thought it was someone else."

It wasn't entirely a lie. This was the last thing she would expect from a man wanted by the law for murder. She squeezed the poster, making it crumble in her hand.

"Here. Allow me."

Oblivious to the paper, he guided her to the table and pulled out a chair for her. She sat, further surprised when he pulled out yet another flower—from where she did not know —and placed it in front of her.

"This was the prettiest one in the field... and it still pales in comparison to your beauty."

Araceli's breath caught. Oh, there had been the occasional shared look before—moments that communicated that perhaps there was something between them. So, this wasn't the first time he had surprised her, but it was definitely a departure from the way he usually spoke. Never before had he straight out said that she was beautiful.

He set a plate of fried chicken down in front of her, boiled potatoes and biscuits accompanying it. In spite of the mess surrounding them, the plate actually looked quite pleasant.

So did he.

His gaze bored into her, making his eyes seem even more piercing...

Like the ones in the poster.

She gave her head a strong shake. "This won't do. It just won't."

His expression fell flat as if all the excitement in him had been a raging fire she effectively doused out with one single statement.

"I'm sorry. Is it the chicken? I could have sworn you said you liked chicken. Maybe it's the way it's cooked. You never did specify what kind. I can remember that for next time, though. I mean, if there is a next time. So, does that mean you like boiled instead?" he blathered on. "Perhaps roasted—"

"No," she said emphatically, waving away the incessant chatter. She stared at him. "The way you look..."

"Do you like it? Your father suggested it might be more suitable."

Her eyes shot hellfire out of them.

"My father?" Had they been available, she would have

thrown every one of her glass jars of paint at him. "How dare you even mention him."

"What?" he asked, confused. "Why? He was the one who thought you might appreciate it if I cleaned up a bit. I'll be honest… I don't mind saying that I enjoy it. I'm kind of feeling like my old self."

Her accent grew thick. "Your old self? Oh, please, tell me about your old self."

Araceli pulled out the crumpled paper and unwrinkled it the best she could. She angrily threw it across the table, but it defied her, softly floating back onto the table and landing neatly in front of him. He stared at it, his face filled with a strange mixture that she couldn't quite peg. Ignorance? Regret? Fear? She couldn't quite say.

"I can explain."

She snorted. "Save your lies for someone with enough fare to buy them. I know who you are. You're that filthy… no good…"

A string of Spanish flew from her lips.

"… American soldier from El Salvado. That's what you are."

"Like I said, if you would just let me explain—"

"What is there that you could possibly say that I don't already know? You're him, are you not? You are the man in the poster… who is wanted for *murder. Sí o no?*"

"Alright. Yes, I'm the man in the poster, but—"

"Murderer."

"I'm not, though. I've never—"

"*Murderer.*"

"Would you stop saying that?"

"Why?"

"Because it's not true!"

"Ha! Now you're going to tell me I didn't see what I saw? You weren't in El Salvado?"

"That's not what I meant. Of course, you saw me. I was there. I just meant that things aren't always as they seem."

"Seems to me you're like any other American soldier who only cared to kill our people so you could steal our land."

"No, I'm not."

"Yes, you are."

"*No*, I'm not."

"*Sí, tu ere—*"

"I'm not even American!"

Araceli stilled, her jaw heavy with shock. She snapped her mouth shut. "What did you just say?"

"I said I'm not American." Araceli's brows shot up with surprise. She looked about ready to say something when Miguel cut her off, shifting uncomfortably. "That's not entirely true, though. I mean, I *am* American. I was born here in this country—same as you. However, my father was from Mexico. I can't right say where since I never had the chance to know him, but maybe now you can see I'm not so different from you."

Araceli's eyes fluttered shut. She tapped the blunted tip of the paintbrush against her temple, considering what he had revealed. Her eyes finally popped open again and she squinted at him, disbelief shining in her bright orbs.

"Do you mean to tell me," she pointed the brush accusingly at him, "that you fought against your own people... *tú raza?*"

"Uh... I was hoping you wouldn't see it like that."

Araceli's head shook with astonishment. "Why would I *not*? Seriously. How could I see it any other way? You've been quietly going along, trying to gain our trust when all this time you've been carrying secrets. Can I believe *anything* you say now, Michael? I mean, is that even your real name?"

"Of course, that's my real name. Well, it is in English anyway. My grandparents insisted on calling me that instead of Miguel... and don't go trying to act all innocent. It's not like I'm the only one keeping secrets around here."

"What are you talking about?" Araceli asked, her voice vexed. "I'm not hiding any secrets!"

"What do you call sneaking out in the middle of the night —dressed like a boy no less? That's how I first met you. Let's not forget how you went back to the forest for those paints, too... Oh, yes. I know you returned *by yourself* even though I asked you to wait because of the danger involved."

"How do you know I went back? Have you been spying on me?"

"What? How could I have done that while I was laid up in bed this whole time?"

"I don't know. Soldiers have sneaky ways."

Miguel let out a frustrated sigh. "That's not true... and stop trying to fall back on the argument of me being a soldier. I'm not anymore. That was in the past—a past that even your father accepts."

"My father?" Araceli asked, incredulously. "I don't believe you."

"It's true."

"Even if it was, I don't care." Her lips began to quiver and her voice broke. "You are a liar and worse... and I never went to see you again."

His voice turned gruff. "You don't mean that."

Araceli abruptly stood and raised the gun.

"Yes, I do. Now, get out of my house."

Standing, Miguel met her challenge. "Go on, then. Skin it if you think you can."

He walked right up to her and pushed his chest into the pistol. Her hand immediately lowered.

"I can't."

He smiled at her confession, which only served to infuriate her more.

"You think something is funny? Huh? You think you can come in here and cook a meal, wash up and look so handsome... and then I'm just going to forgive you?"

His grin grew even wider. "So, you think I'm handsome?"

She grumbled. "Don't try to be cute, because you're not. You hurt my family. You stole our lands and took my brothers. I will *never* forgive you."

Miguel sighed.

"We've been beating this bear for a good while now. I don't know what more I can tell you to make you understand that I'm innocent. That is, I'm guilty of a lot of wrongs in my life. However, I didn't have a hand in what you're accusing me of." He reached out and tucked a wayward strand of loose hair behind her ear. The small touch made her eyes flutter and her breathing slow. "Aw, Chel. I wish you'd believe me. I don't want to wait until I'm some hummingbird before I can kiss my woman."

She came undone at the idea of them belonging to one another, and melted into the curve of his hand against her cheek.

Then images of the past flooded her mind again. She reluctantly pulled away.

"I want to believe you. I really do. I can't unless you have proof, though. Can you prove what you say?"

"I don't know," Miguel said. "You've got my word that I'll try, though. I'd go all the way to Mexico if that's what it took to prove myself to you, Chel."

"I might just hold you to that." She gave him a glimmer of hope, but then snatched it away with the following breath. "Until then, I'm going to have to ask you to leave."

"I really wish you'd reconsider."

"I'm sorry, but I just don't think that it's wise you stay. At least, not until I've spoken with my father."

"Alright. If that's the way you feel about things, then I'll go."

"Thank you."

Miguel calmly ambled out of the room, his gait still plagued with a slight limp. He disappeared from the room, but she could hear him on the steps—up and down again. He reappeared, his satchel swung over one shoulder.

"Well, I guess I better head on out."

She only nodded and followed him to the front door, opening it to show him the way out. He stopped on the porch.

"You know, maybe I was wrong. Maybe the roles are reversed."

"I don't understand."

"You're the one still fighting the battle. I'm the one waiting for you... I always will be."

He turned and left then, leaving her to wrestle with a war of emotions.

CHAPTER 10

*A*raceli paced the office floor back and forth. Two days. That's how long it had been since she ran Michael off.

Michael? Miguel?

Oh, bother. She didn't even know which name to call him by. Not that what name he chose to go by should be her biggest concern at the moment. Equally upsetting was that her father had never made it back home. The first day he failed to return, the men at the mill had seemed unconcerned. Come day two, people were starting to express a bit of unease.

"It was only supposed to be a short trip down the river to see what was causing the back-up," said their foreman, Roberto. "I could see that taking a full day if he decided to clear the area himself. This is a bit alarming, though. What if he was trying to move a log by himself and got trapped under it?"

"Oh, please don't say that." In a rare moment, Araceli crossed herself. "Surely, he wouldn't try to do anything so dangerous."

She knew her words amounted to little more than wishful thinking, though. Her father believed he was still capable of doing the same things he did as a young man. That was what happened at the mill when Michael... Miguel...

Sigh.

When *he* was injured.

"I'm going down there," she decided.

"You can't go by yourself," Roberto insisted. "Besides, it's best to let the sheriff know what's going on. You never know where trouble will pop up."

"You're right," she conceded. "I'll ride into town and get the sheriff. You get a few of the other men and ride on up to the cutoff where the lumber usually gets hung up. We'll meet up with you and keep searching from there."

Men began lining up when Roberto asked for volunteers, one going off to hitch a wagon in case it was needed. Araceli went for her horse. She rode him hard into town, slowing only when she got on Main Street to avoid any accidents with other passerby. She pulled up at what was once the mine's security office, now turned into a sheriff's office with the bedroom transformed into a jail cell. She quickly tied up her horse and marched in, hardly anticipating what she would find.

"You!" She skidded to a halt, shocked to find Miguel sitting on a cot in the ironclad cell. She frowned. "Well, I guess that explains why you never came back."

"What are you talking about?" Miguel stood and strode over to the cell door, easily pushing it open. He laced an arm through one of the bars and leaned against the frame. "I'm just sitting around, waiting for Pete to get back with news."

"Of my father?" Araceli asked, hopeful.

Miguel's brows narrowed. "No... of word regarding my... Wait a minute. What's going on? What's going on?"

Araceli wrung her hands, pacing the small confines of the

sheriff's office. "He never came back. You know, from the day he left? The day you said he was going..." Her eyes grew wide. "You were the last one to see him that day."

"Whoa, now. Just hold on before you go getting any kind of wild thoughts in that pretty little head of yours. You saw me leave out of your place. I was doing good just keeping myself upright. Even now, I'm still having some difficulties getting around. So, there's no way I could have been involved in anything having to do with your father going missing."

"I suppose you're right," Araceli admitted. She didn't add that it was a relief to realize that he couldn't possibly have had anything to do with her father's disappearance. Nor did she mention how thankful she was to see that he was free to come and go of his own accord—meaning that perhaps he really had been telling the truth all along. Of course, that was an issue for a later time. Right now, she had to find out what happened to her father. "Alright. A group of us are going up to the river and search for him. Would you please let Pete know?"

"Are you serious? I'm not sitting here while my future father-in-law is facing possible danger." Araceli's mouth dropped open at his bold statement. Miguel gave her a satisfied nod. "That's right, darling. I'm stating my intentions right now just so you don't get any surprises later on when I prove I'm innocent and ask you all formal like to marry me. Like I said two days ago, I don't want to wait until Heaven to kiss my gal. So, we better get on with the search jack rabbit quick-like."

Miguel strode over to Pete's desk and searched around until he located a piece of charcoal. He looked around for a piece of scrap paper and then pulled open Pete's desk drawer. He pulled out the old wanted poster with his mug on it. "Turns out this thing was useful for something after all."

He scribbled on the back of it, leaving a note as to where

they were going and for Pete to join them as soon as he could. "Alright. Let's go."

They rushed out of the jailhouse.

"That's a nice mare. Where did you get it?" Araceli asked as they each mounted their horses.

"Old man Atherton gave it to me this morning," he said. Then they rode out, silence settling between them until they reached the river. "So, you have an idea where he was heading?"

"About a couple miles downstream," she said. "There's a spot in the river that narrows a good bit. Beavers seem to enjoy picking that particular place to dam up."

"Then I guess that should be our first stop," Miguel said and urged his horse on. However, they only got about halfway to their destination when they saw several of the sawmill workers, a group of Miwok Indians straddling some of the most magnificent horses they had ever seen and...

"Papá!" Araceli raced Inesh up to the group and dismounted, rushing over to the wagon. Her father laid there, unconscious. "What's going on? Is he okay?"

"He will be fine," a young Miwok woman spoke. "We gave him some medicine to help his restless spirit. Now he sleeps."

"Restless spirit?" Miguel asked, dismounting as well. "What's that supposed to mean?"

"They said they found him wandering several miles out," Roberto offered. "Almost like he had been coming from Calderon. He was rambling on, too, about some woman and her brother or husband. Something like that."

"What's Calderon?" Miguel asked.

"The next town over," Araceli said. "If you can call it that. It doesn't have but maybe a couple dozen residents. Still, they somehow manage to survive just fine."

"Well, they said he was clutching this when they found him." Roberto held out a necklace for Araceli to examine. A piece of metal had been fashioned to look like a claw of some sort. In its grip was a stone that looked very much like a ruby shaped into a perfect ball.

"How strange," she said. Then she slipped it into the pocket usually reserved for her six shooter. She walked back over to Inesh and mounted the horse. She addressed the Miwok woman who had spoken earlier. "My apologies, but I didn't catch your name earlier."

"Kela Tukumu."

"Well, thank you, Ms. Tukumu, for taking care of my father in his time of need. What do we owe you?"

The woman gestured with her hand as if running it across a smooth, flat surface. "All debts are paid."

Araceli wanted to say more, but the young woman turned and rode off without a single word more, her party following her.

"I guess they aren't much for talking," Miguel said.

"You wouldn't be either if you had been forced off your land."

"No, I guess not." He looked to change the subject. "That's a mighty fine piece of jewelry. Might want to be careful shoving it in that pocket. It might get scratched up."

"It won't," she promised. "It's the only thing in there right now."

"Really? What about your—"

"I didn't see much point in carrying an empty pistol."

"Empty?" Miguel looked confused, but only for a moment. "You mean to tell me—"

"I never reloaded it after that day of our shooting lessons." She gave him a sheepish grin. "You were never in any real danger during our little... discussion."

He gave her a winning smile. "And yet you lowered it anyway."

"Oh, don't go looking so pleased with yourself. You still haven't proven your innocence."

"I will soon enough. I'm going to ride back into town and let Pete know what's going on."

"We'll ride with you," Araceli offered. "We're closer to town than we are to our house and I'd like Doctor Edwards to take a look at my father—just to make sure he really will be fine. Besides, Ms. Priya's home is on the way and I'm sure she'd like to know what happened."

The group rode on in silence until Priya Dayal's house came into view.

"That's where she lives," Araceli pointed out. She instructed the men, "We'll stop here for a moment and let her know what has happened."

She and Miguel had barely dismounted when two teen girls appeared in the doorway, followed by Priya with a swaddled infant in her arms. Araceli knew of Priya's older girls from her first marriage. However, she was confused as to where the baby had come from. Now wasn't the time for questions, though. She approached Priya and informed her of what had happened.

A worried look crossed the Indian woman's face, making her appear much older than the late thirties Araceli knew her to be. The woman pushed the baby into her arms.

"Here," she said before rushing back into the house. She appeared a minute later, a small bottle of smelling salts in her hands. She made her way to the wagon and opened the vial, waving the salts in front of the resting man's nose. His eyes popped open and he coughed. Priya sighed with relief.

"Thank God, Juan! I was sure something had happened when you didn't come by to kiss the baby goodnight, but I didn't know what to do." She turned to the girls, still standing in the doorway and instructed the oldest. "Go get Bapa's pipe."

"Baby?" Araceli approached, confused. "Bapa? Why does that word sound so much like 'papá?"

Her father slowly sat up in the wagon. He looked first at his daughter and then at Priya who gave him an encouraging nod before turning to the men who had accompanied them. "There is some naan on the table. The girls will show you where you can wash up."

"Thank you, Ms. Dayal," the men chorused and followed her daughters, eager to try the delicious bread. Araceli returned her attention to her father once more, raising a curious brow that stated she waited expectantly for the truth.

"I've wanted to tell you for so long now," he began. "I just didn't know how. I didn't want you to be upset."

"Upset about what?" she asked, straining to keep calm as the daughter appeared with a small object in her hand. Araceli immediately recognized it to be her father's pipe. He took it from the young girl, thanking her with a pat on the head, and lit the tobacco inside. He took a few short puffs off it, exhaling peacefully.

"Chel," he said, "this is my family."

The woods around her spun a little. Araceli felt like she would topple, but Miguel hastily dashed to her side. He straightened her up while Priya took the baby from her arms.

"I don't understand," she said, dazed. "How can this be your family? You already have one."

Señor Arroyo sighed. "Araceli, you will always be my beloved daughter—now and forever. I promise you that. However, your mother has been gone many years now and I don't want to live alone anymore."

"I didn't want to be alone either," Priya added.

"Ms. Dayal was widowed with two young girls to raise and I wanted another chance at life," her father continued. "It only made sense that we should marry."

"Marry?" Araceli asked, looking down at the baby in awe.

He appeared to be only a few months old. "The two of you are married? For how long?"

"A little over a year now."

"And the baby?"

"He is your half-brother, Jagara Dayal Arroyo."

"Brother?" Araceli reached out for the baby, but then pulled back. She looked up at Priya with imploring eyes. "May I?"

The woman smiled broadly at Juan and then his daughter. "Of course you can."

Araceli wrapped her arms around the boy and cuddled him close, breathing in deeply. Tears filled her eyes as she caressed his soft cheeks. "Aw, you smell so sweet. Yes, you do... and so handsome, too. Why, I think you've got my papa's eyes."

The child cooed at her observations.

"You're a natural," Priya declared. "You will do well when you have your own children."

"I couldn't agree more," Miguel said and Araceli was suddenly aware that his arm still rested against her shoulders. She slipped out of his embrace.

"I'm afraid I may never know," she replied and handed the baby back to his mother.

"Why in heavens not?" her father demanded. "Chel, I have seen you attend to this young man for quite some time now. I can understand how you weren't interested in the others, but this one is your perfect match."

"Papá," Araceli discreetly whispered, "how can he be my perfect match when he helped cause all our pain?"

"*Hija*, please, you're not making any sense."

"Don't you understand, papá? He wasn't just a soldier... He's the one who stole our land!"

Her father pulled the pipe out of his mouth. He leaned back in the wagon with a tired sigh and gently folded his hands, resting them on his paunch. "Araceli, where did you get this idea that someone stole our land?"

"What do you mean where did I get the idea? You yourself called the soldiers *ladrones*."

"Yes, *hija*. I did call them thieves, but only because I thought the general had cheated me out of a fair price. In truth, he hadn't. I just wanted a little more."

"What do you mean 'cheated' you? Are you trying to say—"

"That I sold the land."

Stunned, Araceli slowly began to sink once more and, once again, Miguel was there to support her. "You... sold it?"

"Yes, I did. It felt like the right thing to do at the time. Your brothers were gone, as was your sweet mamá, and I didn't see the use in having so much space for just the two of us. Besides, I didn't want to stay in a place with so many sad memories. I thought a change in scenery would be good—for the both of us. So, I sold it. I figured they could have taken it if they wanted to anyway. Better to get some money out of the deal than to lose it for nothing."

"But what about the fire?" she looked up at Miguel.

"I promise I had nothing to do with that."

"He's right," her father confirmed. "That was an act of few spiteful men being unaware that the land had already been sold—just as I had been unaware that your brothers were harboring stolen goods."

"They were?"

"Yes." Her father elaborated, "They stole important documents that had been drafted to end the war. That's why they were executed."

"I never knew," Araceli whispered, horrified by the thought.

"I didn't want you to think less of them. After all, they were your brothers and good men, too. They were just acting under orders from a rogue superior. What more can I say? They were confused."

"I guess we all were," Araceli whispered. She thought back to Miguel and his attempts to make things right… when it had never really been his responsibility to do so. A lump caught in her throat as she thought about all her harsh words. How could he ever forgive such foolish behavior?

"I'm so sorry for the way I've treated you."

"The way you treated me? You mean with homemade meals and painting lessons?"

She smiled at his attempt to lighten the situation, but she wasn't quite ready to forgive herself so easily. "You know what I'm talking about. I should have taken you at your word to begin with."

"Maybe that would have been a little easier to do had I been honest with you from the beginning," he said. "I guess we both learned a little something."

He ran the back of his hand across her brow and then tucked away the one wayward strand of hair that seemed to always escape her pinned braids.

"Looks like we're about to learn something else, too." Señor Arroyo pointed and they all looked up to find Pete coming up the road, a man in a suit and bowler hat riding alongside him. "That man looks like he's got a touch of the law in him."

"There you are," Pete called as he dismounted. "I found your note in my office. Came out as soon as I could. Didn't think to find you all on the road back, though."

"Turns out the men found him easy enough. If he was with a band of Miwok. They apparently found him on his way back from Calderon, mumbling something about a man and woman."

"Calderon?" Pete asked. "What were you doing there, and who were the people you mentioned?"

"I don't really remember," Señor Arroyo said. "It all seems a little hazy."

"Here, papa. You were holding this." Araceli reached into her pocket and pulled out the ruby necklace.

Her father looked thoughtful for a moment.

"Was I? Perhaps I meant it as a wedding gift," he slyly suggested.

"I hope that's going to happen," Miguel said. He nodded to the man in the suit before turning to Pete. "You weren't able to clear my name, were you? Had to bring a magistrate to try me."

Pete and the man exchanged surprised looks. The man gave him a curious grin. "You're mistaken, sir. I'm not here to arrest you. My name's William Mason. I'm here to assign your inheritance."

"My *what?*" Miguel nearly hollered.

"It's true, *amigo.*" Pete gave him a pat on the back. "I followed up on various leads and we found the real killer still hiding out in El Salvado. A guy named Grey—David Grey."

"Grey?"

"Yeah, do you know him?"

"Sure enough. He was under my command when we served. In fact, I heard tale he was involved in the execution of the two Arroyo boys—the soldiers who ransacked a General's tent."

"Yeah, well, two things about that. First, the boys were wrongly charged. They had nothing to do with that."

"My sons were innocent?" Juan Arroyo choked. Both Priya and Araceli reached out to comfort him, but Araceli pulled back when she realized Priya would do well on her own.

"I'm sorry to say, sir, but it seems that way. In fact, a guy named Miller—"

"Moses Miller?" Miguel asked.

"That's right."

"Holy hallelujah… I know him, too.:"

"Well, according to Miller, it was Grey who had turned the tent over. He was determined not to leave the army emptyhanded and penniless. Apparently thought there was some gold to be found there or something. The only thing he found, though, were some documents drafted for the treaty. When he saw someone coming, he knew he'd have to explain the mess. He quickly stuffed the papers in his pants and said that he saw a couple of Mexican soldiers run off. Then Grey buried the papers the first place he could find."

Araceli gasped. "You mean our hacienda?"

"I'm sorry to say," Pete replied.

"It makes sense," Miguel concluded. "We were stationed nearby. It would have been easy to learn who in the area had served in the army."

"And this Grey fellow had said he saw a *couple* of Mexican soldiers," Araceli thoughtfully spoke. "That's why he chose my brothers to pin it on… and the reason my father sold our land."

A fat tear threatened to slide down her round cheek.

Miguel wrapped his arms around her again. This time she melted into his embrace.

"I'm so sorry, Chel. I wish I had known then what I know of Grey now. I'd make sure he hung before getting anywhere near your family."

Araceli looked up, her eyes filled with appreciation. "Thank you," she said, "but I don't think my brothers would want us living with such anger."

"Or sadness," he added and wiped away another tear. The two smiled at one another, affection shining in both their faces. Pete cleared his throat and they quickly pulled apart.

"Well, he'll certainly pay for his crimes now," the sheriff said. "There's going to be a trial."

"And you'll find me there," Miguel volunteered.

"I'm not so sure," Pete said and pointed to the be speckled man who still stood there, silently observing them.

Miguel grinned, sheepishly. "Sorry about that, pal. I almost forgot you were there."

The man smiled kindly. "I hope not, sir. This is quite an inheritance."

"I don't understand how," Miguel admitted. "I'm not in line for anything of the sort."

"Sir, are you or are you not, Michael St. James, also known as Miguel Santiago, the grandson of Daniel and Rebecca Delacroix of the Louisiana Delacroix?"

Delacroix? He never thought he would see the day someone considered him good enough to be part of the family... and certainly not while including his given name in Spanish.

Miguel nodded. "Yes, those are my grandparents."

The man adjusted his spectacles, a hint of melancholy in his tone. "I'm sorry to inform you that those *were* your grandparents, sir. Daniel Delacroix met an untimely death last winter when he took a fall down a flight of stairs. Your grandmother, Rebecca, passed on earlier this month. From the house to all the land, she bequeathed everything to you."

It felt like the world was suddenly off its axis. Miguel's mind reeled with the news.

"Are you sure?"

"Says so right here, sir."

The man held out a pile of documents filled with words that blurred in front of Miguel's face. After all the years that he had been rejected by his mother's family, they had finally accepted him in the end.

Miguel reached out for the papers, but the man pulled them back. "They come with a stipulation, sir."

"A stipulation? What's that?"

"It's here in the letter your grandmother wrote when she was nearing her time."

The man handed over an envelope.

"It's still sealed."

"Yes, sir. She only told me what it was about. She didn't want anyone but you reading it, though. Said it wouldn't be right."

Miguel stuck a finger under the envelope's flap and broke the seal open. He pulled out the letter, a faint fragrance of rosewater wafting towards him, a reminder of childhood days and the perfume that had sat on his mother's desk inside her room, a living mausoleum his grandmother kept of all her daughter's things from before she took her own life. Miguel remembered wandering in once and finding the small glass bottle, liberally spraying its contents on himself before his grandmother stormed in, a look of murder on her face.

He brought the envelope up and inhaled deeply. This small endeavor—his grandmother's inclusion of the sweet, forbidden spray—meant more to him than even the land he had just inherited. He pulled out the letter and unfolded it.

DEAR MIGUEL,

IT MUST COME as something of a shock to see me address you as such. After all the years we insisted upon the name 'Michael,' it almost doesn't seem right to call you anything different. However, that is where I would be wrong.

The truth is, your Christian name was and is Miguel. Your grandfather and I had no right to take away that which your parents gave you. Yes, both of your parents gave you that name. I know we said that your father had run off before you were born, abandoning your mother and you. However, that was a terrible lie. I would ask your forgiveness for the wrong that's been done, but I fear that'll be a task left up to the Maker since I'll surely be gone long before you learn the truth.

The reality is that your grandfather ran him off our land when we learned that he and your mother, our darling, Sophia, had married in secret—the truth coming out only when your mother began to show she was with child. However, your father refused to stay away. So, we shipped your mother off to a convent until after your birth, hopeful that he would believe she was gone forever. When she returned and learned of what happened, she took her own life—another sin I will have to answer for, especially since your father had written her many letters while she was away. Of course, we denied any news from him at all. Then he learned of her death and returned once more. We allowed him to stay for a short while, out of guilt I suppose, and even allowed him to spend time with you until we heard he had secretly baptized you and wanted to take you to Mexico to meet his parents. We were afraid then. We thought he would take yet another from us—that we would never see you again—and we had yet to fill the void from losing our dear daughter. So, your grandfather found some men to help intimidate him, threatening to have him killed. He immediately left and the letters, though growing more infrequent as time went on, never stopped coming.

You will find them along with the title to the Delacroix estate. I have but one requirement before you can claim your inheritance.

I understand now that we stole you from your father. Then we filled your head with lies about him abandoning you. It pains me to admit that there is no prettier way to state those facts, but I'll be cursed to the rotten earth if I don't do all in my power to right such wrongs. I know you always had a love for the land despite your grandfather's insistence that it would never be yours. He was wrong, as was I, and I gladly bequeath all to you provided that you will seek out the father you were denied. Family is so important,

Miguel. I've learned that through the years. I think your grandfa-
ther did as well, but was too stubborn to admit such. So, go find
your family, Michael. Marry well and fill the Delacroix estate with
the love and laughter it never had.

With my contrition, I send my love and blessings in these
regards.

Your Grandmother,
Rebecca Delacroix

STUNNED INTO SILENCE, Miguel slowly folded the letter. All
the years that had gone by not understanding why his father
—and then his aunt—disappeared from his life. It suddenly
all made sense now. His father had been forced to leave by
his grandparents... and probably his aunt as well, if he
thought about it carefully. He was suddenly filled with hope
that maybe they were still alive.

"Wait," he said. "I don't quite understand. What is the stipulation that my grandmother left."

"It's as the letter stated," Mr. Mason explained, "you're to
'fill the Delacroix estate with the love and laughter it never
had.' That begins with marriage."

Miguel smiled down at Araceli. "Well, I don't think that
will be so hard to accomplish."

She blushed slightly. "Are you once again stating your
intentions, Michael... or is it Miguel? Really, I don't even
know how you'd like to be addressed."

Miguel shoved his hands in his pockets and leaned back
against the tree as though it's strong foundation was enough
to support all the turmoil inside. He considered her words
carefully. No one had ever actually asked him what he would

like to be called. Then again, it wasn't like anyone had known there was an option. It was an oversight he was determined to remedy.

"My parents gave me the name Miguel. I think they made a wise choice."

"Then I accept your proposal, Miguel."

"Well, someone's awfully confident. I haven't even asked yet," he teased.

"Oh, but you will," she challenged.

"And the sooner the better," Mr. Mason interrupted. He pulled out another document. "You have to say 'I do' by your thirtieth birthday."

"What?" Miguel asked. "But that's next week! That's not enough time to plan a wedding."

Priya laughed. "You don't know the ladies in this town— or Atherton Winslet. He could get a wedding done in a day if need be."

"Believe us," Araceli's father chimed in. "We speak from experience. Besides, who do you think it was who suggested the two of you *might* make a good match?"

"Mr. Winslet?" Araceli asked, surprised. Although, she shouldn't have been. From what she knew of the man, he did consider himself something of a matchmaker.

"Then it sounds like we might have a wedding to prepare for," Miguel said. He pulled Araceli away from the others, near a grove of trees so they could speak privately. Then he kneeled before her. "That is, if you'll have me."

She joined him, not giving a whit about her skirts getting covered in dirt.

"I don't see any reason to fight it any longer," she said.

Then she waited until his mouth claimed hers, thankful that they didn't have to wait to share their first kiss because their love wasn't the end of some legend.

It was the beginning of one.

A LETTER TO READERS

I hope you enjoyed reading about Araceli and Miguel. As some of you may already know, I have the tendency to write about lost identity—the questioning of who we are and what our potential might be. I think a lot of that stems from my own childhood and mixed heritage. I never quite knew where I fit in, and I tried hard to be someone I wasn't because of it. That's what I was hoping to convey when I wrote Miguel's character. Yep! For the first time ever, I actually wrote myself in as the hero instead of the heroine. Well, maybe there's a little bit of me in the heroine too.

If you enjoyed reading *Dueling the Desperado*, then I think you will appreciate the next book in the series by author Dallis Adams, *Sweeten the Swindler.* Turn the page to get an exclusive excerpt not found anywhere else. Then stick around to read yet another passage—this one from my Spanish rendition of Cinderella, entitled *A Royal Decree.*

As always, thanks for reading!

Paz y bendiciones...

A LETTER TO READERS

(Peace and blessings)

~ Mimi ~

SWEETEN THE SWINDLER

Can a swindler convince a stickler
her life is a lie?

DALLIS ADAMS

The earth shifted beneath Maxine Sweeten's feet, causing her stomach to lurch. A cry from her mother split the air, followed by her father's shout. Then her beloved parents disappeared over the cliff into nothingness, leaving only blue sky.

Heart lurching, she scrambled backward, trying to gain purchase, to grab onto something. Anything. But rocks and dirt crumbled around her. She fell on her backside. In a last, desperate act, she twisted and made a lunge for some sagebrush, hoping it would support her small eleven-year-old body.

Dirt continued to rain on her face as it fell into the hungry canyon, but the tough, wiry brush held. She blinked the soil from her eyes and looked down. A small ledge protruded by her calves. Lifting her feet, she managed to stand on the narrow protrusion. But she shook so badly that she decided to keep clinging to the brush.

"Mum? Da?" Her voice called back to her several times from the bowels of the gorge and then died. She looked over her shoulder. The bottomless canyon yawned in the darkness, as if it were still famished. She shivered.

Did they live? Were they lying far below, hurt?

No.

In her heart, she knew they had not survived.

A keening wail rent the air. She wondered what kind of animal could make that sound, but then realized she was the one who was caterwauling. Finally her tears subsided. Her hands ached. She still held the brush, so tightly her knuckles were white. She took several breaths, willing her brain to work.

What would Da do if he were in her shoes? He was a naturalist and loved to travel for the magazine he'd founded —*American Nature*. He'd known so much about botany, geology and ethology. It was the latter—the study of animals and their behavior—that interested Maxine the most. Her Da believed she'd inherited her great grandma's ability to communicate with them.

The setting sun bathed her in pink and orange hues. Soon it would be dark. She heard a rustle. Then a scurrying of small feet. She wasn't alone.

You have an affinity with animals, Maxine. Trust your instincts.

She glanced up and saw large antlers first, ones that curled back. Then dark eyes surrounded by white gazed down at her. A bighorn sheep. The surefooted animal climbed down toward the sagebrush to which she still clung and then—amazingly—knelt next to her.

As she climbed onto its back, she made a promise to herself. She would always look after the wild animals of the land, no matter where she ended up living.

Continue reading here

Of all the rotten luck!

"You don't understand. I *am* the daughter of Vicente de Zapatero."

The guards threw back their heads with laughter.

"And I'm the bloody Count del Castillo," one wheezed with mirth.

Elena firmly planted both fists on her hips. "You mock me, sir. However, I speak the truth. If you would only go inside and—"

"Now see here, you foul little *zorra*..."

Elena gasped.

"... We've had enough with the likes of you. The *fiesta* is by invitation only. Unless you can produce one, you're not getting in. Neither are the rest of the wanton workers who keep wandering this way. The Count wants a wife – not whatever disease you and your ilk obviously carry. Now get out of here before we arrest you!"

Elena bit back a retort. The last thing she wanted was to land in a *carcel*, trapped behind thick iron bars set in solid stone. She gathered her skirts with a distinct *"humph"* and gave the guards one last glare before moving along. She wandered away, waiting until she had rounded the corner and was free to feel along the tall stone wall.

There has to be another way in!

Yet the only thing in view was a lush orange tree, its branches heavy with ripe fruit. She had heard tales of the trees surrounding the House of Castillo. It was common knowledge that on the day of "Passing the Peerage," the superseding noble was to authorize a new law. Typically, it was something that taxed the villagers and they were required to give a greater portion of their grain or donate livestock. Naturally, there would be quiet complaints amongst the townsfolk – criticisms that would die on the tips of their tongues before reaching the powerful nobility who could create costlier, even fatal conditions. However, such had not been the case with the last señor. In a moment of rare generosity, the late Conde del Castillo had ordered the trees planted in an attempt to feed the poorest of the villagers. Each family was allowed one orange apiece, encouraged to sow the seeds and nurture the soil it claimed, the hope being that it would eventually take root.

Hence the explanation of this sole climber standing like an unwounded soldier loaded with ammunition. Elena leaned against it, welcoming the cool shade its canopy offered. She slowly slid down the trunk, plopping onto the cool grass below with a soft thud. The moment's rest gave her time to examine her bare feet, bloody and sore from the long walk into town. If she thought they looked bad now, she could only manage what was to be expected once the blisters turned into callouses. She grimaced. Oh, well. They would look terrible, but at least she had saved the shoes. Smiling, she patted the hidden pocket sewn in her skirt, proud of the little secret held there. She glanced around, ensuring there were no witnesses present. When all appeared safe, she reached into the pouch and pulled out one of the delicate slippers. Encrusted with precious jewels her father had spent years to procure, it gleamed in the sun like a promise.

Better days awaited her.

She carefully balanced the shoe in one hand, bringing it close to her face so she could examine the intricate pattern designed so that each gem would catch and reflect the maximum amount of light imaginable. She had to admit that while she was a good shoemaker, she had yet to obtain the craftsmanship her father had effortlessly produced. The thought of him and the news she was to deliver to her stepmother brought on an episode of fresh tears. Openly weeping, she clutched the slipper to her chest, intent on having herself a good cry until the snapping sound of a branch overhead caused her to look up.

"Hola, hermosa."

Elena screamed, the outcry startling a man poised on one

slender branch, his arms desperately flapping up and down. However, the more he flailed the weaker his balance grew until he, predictably, landed with a solid thud beside her, moaning as if his ill fate was the worst that could happen to a body. Then (as if that were not enough to confirm this day was truly the most miserable of them all) an orange bounced off her head and rolled onto the ground.

"Ouch!" Elena slapped a hand to her russet crown. Ignoring the man's continued groans, she reached over to where the fruit had landed, digging into its flesh with a gripe. "Ammunition indeed. I'll undoubtedly find a goose egg growing in the morning."

"I would be so fortunate to suffer so little," the man said as he sat upright. "I'll surely have bruises from head to toe."

"Serves you right," Elena retorted. She tried to ignore the way jet-black curls framed a strong face with coffee colored eyes that welcomed any onlooker to drown in them. "What kind of decent man does something as foolish as climb trees? Only a thief attempting to take more than his allotted share."

"I am no thief."

"Then why would you not pick the fruit from one of the lower branches?"

"Because I was not as interested in picking oranges as I was hiding from the calculating mothers of hopeful daughters determined to make a fine match with anyone positioned to secure their station."

It took her a moment to fully appreciate the implication made. When she did, she was quick to bow her head. "My apologies, *señor*. I didn't realize you were with the *nobleza*. Please forgive my loose tongue."

"Nonsense. There's nothing to forgive. In fact, I should probably be thanking you for your attempt to guard this sacred tree of forbidden fruit. After all, it is the only one in the entire village – possibly in all of Spain."

A rueful smile tugged at the corner of his mouth and she knew he was teasing her. Well, if that was the way he wished to play, he would soon learn that games were not only for the gentry.

"Oh, I see. You *are* with the royal court... as their *payaso*."

The man laughed and then stuck out his chest with pride. "Indeed. I am not only the jester, but I am the king of them all. Well, maybe not *el rey* himself. There may be one or two humorous sorts who could best me yet. Let us settle with the Count of Jesters. *De acuerdo?*"

"You're a curious man," Elena said, unsure exactly what to make of his unconventional, but jovial ways.

"And you are a shoeless woman," he replied.

Elena glanced down to her feet. Suddenly embarrassed, she pulled them in and they disappeared under her dress. Attempting to demonstrate that she was not bothered by her own unusual manner, she gave a careless shrug. "I wanted to save my slippers."

"And what an exquisite creation it is. May I?" The man reached for the shoe, plucking it up before she could respond. Then he grasped one tired foot from beneath her dusty hem, lifted it up and gently slipped the bejeweled masterpiece over her toes. "There it is. A perfect fit."

Follow the story here...